A Hood Virgin & A Down South Billionaire

An Urban Novel

Shontaiye Moore

A Hood Virgin & A Down South Billionaire

Published in the United States of America.

Published by Cole Hart Signature, LLC.

Mailing List

To stay up to date on new releases, plus get information on contests, sneak peeks, and more,

Go To The Website Below…

www.colehartsignature.com

Chapter 1
Cashmere "Cash" Ellis
Atlanta, GA

2013

The stench of fresh urine reached my nostrils as it puddled onto the carpet and seeped down into its fibers. It had been a while since I'd had an accident, but fear had reunited me with an old habit I could never seem to shake. I was so scared I wanted to cry. We all were, but we had been told not to 'make a fuckin' sound.' That was exactly what the tall, skinny man turned to us and yelled after he knocked my mama down and ran into the house with a short, fat man right behind him.

While the skinny man screamed and pointed a gun in my mama's face, the fat man ran into the back where my daddy was. They had black masks that covered their faces, but we could still see their eyes and lips. Although, that didn't too much matter because I still didn't know who either of the men were. Didn't recognize their voices either. What did stick out to me was that the skinny man was unusually tall. Taller than anyone I'd ever seen in real life anyway.

Tears wet my own eyes seeing my mama cry. The skinny man had a fistful of her hair and had hit her over the top of the head with the gun he was holding. I knew it hurt my mama badly because her scream was so loud that it caused my small body to tremble with fear.

The fat man had already pushed my daddy through the door of the spare room of our three-bedroom house. It was small and right across from the entrance to the living room and directly beside my parents' room. My siblings and I all shared a room. Although we were in the living room, I could still see and hear my daddy and the man. They were right by the door and from what I saw and heard, my daddy had been doing everything that the fat man asked. He moved when he said move, took him to the safe that he kept in the room, and had even put the code in to lock it. Only after hearing my mama be hit did he start fighting. It didn't go well for him, because as soon as he swung, the fat man started whipping his ass. I knew what an ass whipping looked like because every now and then we got them. Plus, I'd seen my daddy give them to a few guys on the streets after an argument or if they owed him some money. With his chubby arm going up and down, the fat man brought his gun against my daddy's head over and over.

"In the room! Now!" the skinny man demanded before approaching and towering over us.

He'd left my mama bleeding on the kitchen floor and pushed us into the first bedroom he saw. It was my parents' room. A place where we'd normally beg to enter now seemed like a cage.

"All three of y'all, lay down on yo' stomach and close yo' fucking eyes and don't make a fuckin' sound."

We dropped to the floor quickly and lay flat on our tummies. Those were his final and only instructions before shutting the door to the room. A few seconds passed since the skinny man closed us in, and I found myself silently praying for the moment that we could get up and finish watching our movie. Odd thoughts despite the circumstances, but they were my thoughts.

Frozen *had recently been released, and although it was a girl's movie, my brother Nook was just as happy to be watching it as we were. Trying not to be selfish, I also prayed that my mama and daddy were okay. I was young, but I was old enough to sense danger. And I had no doubt that the two men were dangerous.*

"I want Mommy," my brother Nook cried, interrupting my prayer.

He was seven and the baby out the three of us. I was eight and Satin was nine.

"Shhhh!" I hushed him sharply. "Shut up before he comes back."

Nook was notorious for getting us in trouble, but I wasn't having it that day. I was scared of what would happen if we didn't do what we were told. I didn't want to find out either.

"Yeah, shut up Nook," Satin cosigned, her voice trembling.

We were still on our bellies, lying on the floor. I was on one side and Nook was on the other. Satin lay in between us. Of course, none of us were able to see, so we just listened.

"Where the rest of it?" the skinny man yelled in the living room.

They continued to argue, although at times, I couldn't quite make out what they were saying. The two men had been inside our home for a few minutes and whatever they were searching for, they couldn't seem to find.

"Th-th-that's it. I swear to God, man!" my dad whined weakly in a voice that I didn't recognize coming from him.

He sounded scared and I'd never seen or heard him scared before. My daddy was the strongest. The bravest. And normally it was other folks' voices trembling with fear when they talked to him. Never my daddy's.

"Nigga, you said you knew for a fact he was holding. You said you had a good fuckin' source. We came all the way up here for this bullshit. A thousand fuckin' dollars! You cracked the safe open just to pull out this bullshit!"

This time it was the fat man speaking. His voice was deep and scary, while the skinny man spoke quick, his voice shaking as he talked.

"Smoke this nigga," the big man demanded calmly.

"What?"

"You heard me," he repeated.

"Come on, man. That's not what we came here for. Let's just take what they got and go," the skinny man argued desperately. I wasn't sure what smoke meant, but whatever it was, it didn't sound good because he didn't seem to want to do it.

"It's them or you ... and the way I'm feeling right now, it might just be them ... and you. Now I ain't gon' repeat my motherfuckin' self."

The room seemed to go quiet and then the skinny man finally replied.

"Man, I ain't come here for all that. I ain't killin' nobody. I'm here to save a life, not take one."

There was a brief moment of silence and then ...

"Please no!" my mama screamed.

Pop!

My mama screamed again. This time louder.

"Noooooo! Bobby! Baby, please! Get up, baby!" she hollered in a voice that I'd never heard from her before.

Hearing that loud pop and then my mama screaming and hollering, caused all three of us to fall into a fit of tears. Something was wrong and we were now terrified. Too scared to move, open our eyes, or go check. All we knew was that the two men were bad, and we didn't want them opening the door to where we were and doing anything to us. Even though we were laying on the floor, we found a way to get closer to one another for comfort. Meanwhile, my mama was still screaming, and the man was still yelling.

"Bitch, shut the fuck up!" the fat man yelled over and over. "Shut this bitch up right now!"

"Angie, please stop all that screaming," the skinny man begged, but my mama didn't quiet up. Whatever had happened to my daddy had her throwing a fit.

"What the hell is wrong with you bruh!" tall and skinny yelled above my mama's screams.

"Ain't shit wrong with me, and I ain't mean ask her. I meant make her, nigga."

"Fuck that shit, man! We ain't come here for that! I'm not doing it!" the skinny man argued. "I can't!"

The fat man laughed. "Of course, you can't."

Pop! There was another thud.

"What the hell, man!" the skinny man yelled.

"Quiet yo' ass down. You knew what type of nigga I was when you asked for my help. You told me it was gon' be at least twenty thousand in here. This mufucka had one funky ass grand and a bunch of jewelry we gon' have to sell for the low. These niggas running round like they rich and shit. Where I'm from, you always keep enough bread on hand to satisfy a hungry nigga if you ever get robbed. Pump faking will get you popped. Now come on, grab that jewelry and let's get the fuck on."

No more words were exchanged. I heard a bunch of moving around and heavy footsteps. Only when the screen door slammed shut did I know that the bad men were gone. Despite that, we kept quiet and remained still. We were still too scared to move because we weren't sure if the men were coming back. With the three of us scared to speak, it was deathly quiet. My mama and daddy's voice had long been silenced. Nook may not have known, but Satin and I knew something had happened to them and in a sense, none of us were ready to face it. So, we waited.

For days, we didn't eat anything or drink anything. We didn't even get up to use the bathroom. We held it for as long as we could and when that didn't work, we did our business right where we lay at. After a while, the strong putrid scent of pee filled the room, eventually fading as our noses adapted to it.

Eventually, my daddy's friend Buster would come by. We called him Uncle Buster because he and my daddy were so close that he was like an uncle to us. I guess he knew something was wrong because after banging on the door for a while, he kicked it in and came inside. It was then that we finally felt safe enough to get up. The sound of Uncle Buster's sobs confirmed that something bad had happened to our mama and daddy. His cries confirmed his devastation. My siblings and I were all scared but at the time, we didn't understand completely. We'd heard the gunshots, but our little minds wouldn't be able to absorb right away that our mother and father had been shot and killed. We didn't understand how much our lives would be impacted by the tragedy.

My mama and daddy were unrecognizable. The burn marks from the bullets were in their chests, but the way their entire bodies looked would forever be a stain in my memory. I would never forget seeing them that way.

Uncle Buster had tried to keep us from seeing them, but he was so upset, he didn't notice me sneaking a peek. My mama was a petite woman, and my daddy was short and stocky; however, that day, both of their bodies were nearly twice their regular size. Tight and swollen with skin that looked more greenish than brown.

Nook would go wail in a corner, while Satin and I would sit on the couch and find comfort in each other's arms. She cried because she probably knew that it was bad for us. I, however, didn't shed a tear. I was simply numb. Shocked by what we'd heard and what we'd just witnessed. Things were sinking in, and it was only because of Uncle Buster's reaction.

According to one of the officers that arrived, our parents had been dead around thirty-six hours. I had no idea that we had even been lying on the floor that long. That was the day our lives would change. We had just moved to Atlanta. The day we'd go from a comfortable, normal life into a new one like we'd never seen.

Chapter 2
Ezekiel "Wolf" Griffin
Decatur, GA

48 hours later

"Mama, you okay?" I asked through the crack of the closed bathroom door.

I'd jumped out of bed when I heard her heaving up the lining of her stomach. Couldn't have been much more since she barely ate anything these days.

"You okay?" I repeated, when I didn't get an answer after a few seconds.

"I'm fine, baby. Go back to bed, you got school in the morning," she croaked weakly.

Her usually warm, syrupy voice was now hoarse and weak. It was just like her to think of us when she was feeling her worse.

"Yes ma'am."

Despite my words, I turned the knob of the door, but it was locked. Hesitating, I eventually walked away slowly. All I wanted to do was wrap her in my arms like she did when I was sick. I wanted to hug her, kiss her bald head, and tell her that it would be okay. I just wanted to be there for her, but because of her African heritage, she'd been raised strong, and unless it was absolutely out of her control, then she hated showing any signs of weakness. When it was all said and done, she wanted me and my sister to remember her at her best. My daddy always told her to stop talking like that. That we wouldn't need to remember her because she wasn't going anywhere, and he was going to make sure of that.

Since my mama had been diagnosed with cancer six months back, he'd been doing any and everything he could to bring in extra money. Working overtime and any odd job that he could, it didn't matter what it was.

The insurance provided by the beef plant that he and my mama had worked at for the last ten years didn't cover all the meds she needed for her treatment, and the doctors said that she would feel more pain without them. They weren't lying either. After seeing and hearing my mother scream for Jesus a few nights, he vowed that he would work, day and night, to make sure she had everything she needed. The ones that we couldn't afford. After all, she had given up so much for him. For us.

I climbed back into my twin-sized bed after leaving my mama in the bathroom. I didn't bother shutting my eyes. I just stared at the ceiling, while my feet dangled slightly over the side of the bed. Knowing my mama was up and in pain made it harder to sleep. After about ten minutes of counting the circles in the aging popcorn ceiling, I heard the light taps of my mama's footsteps through the hallway as she went back to bed. That, of course, helped me drift to sleep since I felt better knowing that she was in a little less pain than earlier. I loved my mama with every piece of me and I didn't know what my sister and I would do without her.

* * *

"Daddy! That you?" I yelled out several hours later into the darkness.

Apparently, I had fallen into a deep sleep but had been woken abruptly by a loud bang. It was so forceful that it snatched me right up. As expected, I was disoriented but I blinked quickly to shake off the sleep. I called out into the darkness again, this time a little louder just in case he didn't hear me.

I figured it was my daddy since lately he had been coming in later and later. Most nights he was quiet, but every now and then he would drop something or bump into something that would wake somebody, if not everybody, up in the house.

"Daddy! Is that you?" I called out again.

I waited. For several seconds there was nothing, and then things took a turn and quickly began to unfold.

There were footsteps. Several. My mind began swirling with questions. Had my daddy brought someone home with him? Was someone trying to break in? I wasn't sure, but I was about to get up and check.

I wiped my eyes and swung my feet around to climb off the bed. Before I was fully able to do that, a chill flowed through my body as I heard my sister let out a piercing scream. I quickly stood at my feet but by the time I could take a step, my bedroom door flung open. I parted my lips to speak but stopped. I froze at the sight in front of me. There was a man at my door holding a double-barrel shotgun and he had it pointed in my face. I swallowed the hard lump in my throat while my eyes remained fixed on the intruder.

My daddy taught me a lot about guns. He used to have several but had sold them to get money. He now only had one. One that he kept on him. How I wished it were available. Since I knew a little about guns, I knew how powerful the one the man was holding was. I knew that I needed to comply because if I got hit with what he was holding, my death would be certain.

I took in slow, deliberate breaths as I eyed the man cautiously. Wondering why he was in our home.

"I got him!" the man called out.

He was a skinny guy, with beady eyes and a raggedy beard and smooth cut near the front of his head. Although he wore no mask and I could clearly see his face, I didn't recognize him. Had never seen him around before or ever in my life.

"Bring 'em out," the other guy called out.

With the gun still held steady in the air, the man did a little side nod motion with his head for me to move. I quickly obeyed and cautiously made my way past him and through the living room. The entire time I walked through the hall, I braced myself for the powerful impact of the gun. I was anxious and the adrenaline flowing through me had my heart racing. All that was going through my head was that he was going to shoot me in the back.

"Where my mama and sister?" I found the courage to ask.

Neither were in the living room, and I wanted to make sure they were okay. The crazy part was, I wasn't scared. Nervous maybe, but not scared.

"Shut the fuck up, lil' nigga. You don't ask no questions. You only answer them."

My eyes followed the voice to the hall. It was no longer the man with the double-barrel shotgun talking. There was a second man. He had emerged from the back and now walked toward me, anger flickering in his eyes. It was dark but I could see it. They were there to do harm. Looking past the man, I glanced down the hall nervously. My mama and sister were still in the back and were no longer screaming. I glanced up as the man now stood directly in front of me. I was tall for my age, but he was taller. He nearly towered over me. His medium-thick build kind of reminded me of the rapper Slim Thug.

"We lookin' for yo' pops, Charles. Where he at?" he continued sternly.

His voice was deep and angry. My daddy worked day and night. I wasn't sure what he could have done to the men to make them so angry. His dark eyes pierced into me while he waited for a response.

"He ain't here," I stammered.

My eyes cut to the hallway again. Still no sound from my mama or sister.

"No shit," the man countered sarcastically. "We can see that. So, where he at?" the man continued. "It's damn near two in the morning. Where the fuck could the nigga be at? Who could he be with?"

I wasn't sure where he was, but I had an idea of who he was with. My daddy had a brother named Paul. They'd been inseparable growing up but began drifting away from one another as they got older. Uncle Paul stayed in some shit while my daddy was a more peaceful man. Throughout the town, Uncle Paul was known as bad news, but despite the rumors, my daddy still loved his brother.

My uncle was in and out of town, often staying in the Atlanta area. When he came through, my dad still kept in touch with him and hung out with him from time to time. Over the last few weeks, he'd been around more often than usual. Uncle Paul had a temper, liked to fight, stole from people, and had a terrible drinking habit. None of that stopped my daddy from looking up to and hanging out with his big brother. My daddy also had a homie named James, and if he wasn't with him, then he was with my uncle Paul.

Where could he be at? The question sounded in my head again like an alarm.

"I-I don't know," I lied.

I was only thirteen, but I was old and wise enough to know that the men were bad news, and I wasn't about to tell them shit.

After I replied, the man stared at me for a few seconds and then an evil smile spread across his face right before he drew his fist back and drove it dead into the middle of my face. I heard a crack as pain exploded through my entire head as I crumpled to the ground. Blood rushed from my nose and mouth and ran onto the hardwood floor where I now lay. Out of instinct, my hand went to my nose where the bleeding was heaviest. I had a feeling he'd broken it. I gently cupped it and applied pressure while I moaned in agony. With zero sympathy, the man continued talking.

"You see ... I tried to give yo' little bitch ass the benefit of the doubt. A nigga like me done already done his research. I know exactly who yo' daddy run with, and so do you. I wanted to see if I could trust you just a little bit. See if yo' word meant something. But I see it don't."

I didn't bother to respond. All I could focus on was the pain I was in. I'd stopped all the moaning. All that did was make me look weaker and I didn't want to give the nigga the satisfaction. He'd already knocked blood out of me. I wasn't about to give his ass no tears and cries to go with it.

"You let yo' hoe-ass daddy know that I'm looking for him. He knows why I'm here. And I won't stop 'til I run into him and that bitch-ass brother of his."

"Come on, Loco," he said to the man still holding the shotgun.

I held onto the name and promised myself I wouldn't forget it.

"Ay yo, Chris and E! Let's go!" the tall man said.

I now knew that there were four of them in total. And I had all their names. All except the ringleader. The ones I did have would stain my memory until I forced them away.

"Aw man, already? We can't have no fun?" he asked jokingly.

"Man, ain't nobody here for that," Loco said, his face twisting into a scowl. "They try that bullshit every time we put in work and run across some bitches," he complained.

The tall man chuckled and shrugged.

"To each his own. Anything goes when revenge is involved," he replied to Loco.

"Make it quick!"

It was at that moment that I knew what they were about to do. Face still bloody and in a panic-induced frenzy, I scrambled to get up, but the tall man stopped me by crashing his boot down against my face repeatedly until I was unconscious.

Chapter 3
Cashmere Ellis

Eight years later

"Y'all chilren gon' learn 'bout stealing out my damn sto'!"

The stern message carried by a deep southern drawl stopped me in my tracks as I did exactly what she accused me of. Before I could shuffle my feet to take flight, a pair of strong hands grabbed a fistful of my collar and spun me around. My face twisted into an angry scowl as I was brought face-to-face with the old, fat ass lady that apparently owned the place. Although I would have never guessed it, because she worked behind the counter like everybody else.

"Get off me!" I demanded, although it came out more like a whine.

I tried to pull and shake from her grip, but it grew tighter the more I resisted. My eyes darted around, searching for my partner in crime, but I couldn't find my sister Satin anywhere.

"Ain't no need looking for that gal. She took off as soon as she saw me reach to grab yo' little thieving ass. Y'all come in here every week taking shit. Let me see what you got," she demanded as she pulled me closer and glared at me through dark eyes.

I sighed defiantly, and with an attitude, let the stolen items I had tucked inside my dingy, tattered jacket fall to the floor. If she wanted to see, then she could bend down and pick it up herself. Before the satisfied smirk could creep to my face, the bitch let go of my collar and gripped the back of my neck, forcing me down to the floor to pick up the shit I had dropped.

"Get it up and hand it to me heathen, before I tear the fur off yo' ass. You got the right one today!"

While she waited for me to comply, she evilly dug her fingers deep into the sides of my neck until they couldn't go any further. It hurt worse than the slipper that my grandmama would tag our ass with every now and then, so in pain and being held against my will, I did as I was told. I figured my defiance was just going to make her worse, so it was better for me to just do what she said. Even though my face was still bawled up, my eyes had begun pooling with tears.

I was upset for three reasons. One, I was caught and was now embarrassed, two, the bitch was hurting me, and three, I no longer had any of the things I needed for me and my siblings. Basic necessities that folks took for granted, we were out there stealing on a weekly basis.

After rising back up from the floor, I handed her the three items I'd taken. As soon as she saw them, I watched her eyes immediately soften, and then after standing there for a while in thought, she slowly released my neck.

"How old is you, gal?" she asked as she took the crackers, cans of potted meat, and sanitary pads from my hand."

"Sixteen," I grumbled while swallowing the sobs that wanted to come out.

"Ain't yo' mama ever told you it wasn't good to steal from people?"

She placed the items on the closest rack and waited for a response.

"I ain't got no mama. She dead," I finally replied angrily. "Daddy too."

"That still don't make stealing right. Who you stay wit'?" she asked me.

With my mug curled up, I remained silent.

"Gal, I'm 'bout five seconds from beating the black off you if you don't answer my damn question," she said sternly.

Where I was from, the old folks would beat each other's kids like their own, so I took her threat seriously. I was sixteen but I was small. I stood around 5'3 and I was what many considered underweight. I believed her when she said she would beat my ass, and I wasn't about to try and tussle with her. She was the stereotypical older lady from the south. Heavy-set and busty, with roller-curled gray hair and a faded apron.

"I stay with my grandmama," I finally mumbled.

I had my reasons for not wanting to tell her who I lived with. My grandma's health was deteriorating so it wasn't like I was scared that she was gon' give out a whooping. It had been a long time since I'd gotten one of those. No, she was too old and far too weak for all that. Back when we were younger, she used to fuss us out, but these days she barely had the strength to hold a conversation. We practically cared for ourselves. My grandmama had done the best she could and the last thing she needed was someone popping up at her house to tell her that we were out stealing basic necessities like food and sanitary napkins.

"Well, let's go," the lady said. "You coming with me and I'm taking you home so I can tell yo' grandmammy how you and that other girl been stealing up out of here every chance y'all get. I've been watching both of you for a while now. Maybe she'll put something on y'all ass, so I won't have to."

"Ma'am please, don't tell on us," I replied desperately. "My grandmama sick and we struggling."

"We all struggle sometimes," she responded with zero sympathy. "I've struggled before but I ain't never stole from nobody."

My eyes began pooling with tears. Of course, I had other reasons for not wanting her to go to my grandmama's house. She was bedridden so that meant if someone stopped by, she would try to invite them in to talk. My grandmama had lived the way she lived so long that her living conditions were normal to her, even though they wouldn't be to someone else. To put it mildly, we lived fucked up and I didn't want anybody to see it. For that reason, we never had company. There was no company to have. It was me, my brother, and my sister. Just the three of us and my grandmama. It had been that way for a long time. I let the tears roll, took a deep breath, and began pleading with the lady.

"Look ma'am, I know it's not right to steal and I'm sorry. I stole the food so we would have something to eat tonight and tomorrow," I said between sobs. "We don't really eat much so I figured the crackers and stuff would last us for a few days. I got the pads because me and my sister bleeding and we don't got nothing to use. My grandmama stay in the bed sick, so we really just tryin' to make it the best way we can," I admitted.

The tears were really running at this point. I was ashamed and I was desperate. I had never told an adult any of the things I'd just told her, but for some reason, underneath the rock-hard visage, the lady seemed kind and forgiving. And after standing there and crying for another ten seconds, I found out that I was right. The lady sighed and I knew that she was going to help.

"What's yo' name, gal?" she asked.

"Cashmere, but everybody calls me Cash." I sniffled gently.

"Cash, huh. You said yo' mama and daddy dead?"

I nodded, using the back of my arm to wipe away the snot that had run down from my nose and accumulated above my lip.

"What's yo' grandmama name?"

"Betty," I said to her.

I noticed her brows go up.

"That stay in the teeny yellow house on Dudley Road?"

I nodded again. I took it that she knew my grandmama.

"So, you a Dupont?"

"Yes ma'am. My mama was, but my daddy was an Ellis. I got his last name."

"I see."

She paused for a few seconds, staring at me oddly. After a deep sigh, she continued.

"From now on, you call me Fat Mama. That's what errbody call me. That, or they just shorten it to Fat Ma. They all knows me 'round here, and they know one thing I don't tolerate is disrespect. *Or stealing*." Her tone had changed and although it was still stern, it had softened considerably.

"Don't care how bad off you is. You don't take from people," she continued. "We gon' leave the past in the past tho'. We'll get along just fine. Long as you don't ever steal, disrespect me, and long as you don't ever lie to me. Ya hear?"

I mumbled a 'yes ma'am' while she kept on talking.

"I knows you were struggling by the things you took. But you gave me a nasty little attitude and Fat Mama believes in ... how the young folk say it? *Returning energy*."

She looked down at my tear-stained face while I stood there apologetically. Me and my sister weren't bad people, we just didn't want to keep going without. I wanted to tell her that, but deep in my heart, I had a feeling that I didn't need to explain it because she could sense it.

"I see you shamed and seem sorry about what you did, so we gon' move past all that and start over, ya hear?"

"Yes ma'am. I mean Fat Mama." I sniffled and instead of my arm, this time used the back of my hand to wipe my nose as clean as I could.

Fat Ma grabbed the meat, crackers, and pads off the shelf and handed them back to me.

"Thank you," I said, as I eagerly accepted everything.

"Mmm hmm. What grade you in?" she asked.

"Eleventh," I said, a bit more cheerily. I couldn't lie, my heart was swelling with gratitude.

"Eleventh? You's a tiny little thing, ain't you? You said you sixteen?"

"Yes."

"Well, I'll tell you what, be here Monday when school let out, four o'clock sharp. I'm gon' give you a job. You can work for me here. That way you'll have a chance to earn yo' own money and learn a few thangs. So you don't keep running around like a hooligan, stealing from folks."

"Yes ma'am, and thank you ma'am. Uh, I mean, Fat Mama."

"Mmm hmm," she replied with a nod. "And let that other gal know that I'm gon' get with her when I see her. Might even kick her ass."

"Yes ma'am."

"Four o'clock sharp! Don't you be a minute late," she reminded me as she walked away from me and headed back up to the counter.

With the items given to me up against my body securely, I scurried out of the store and high-tailed it back home. During the quick walk, I couldn't help but think about how easily I'd been let off the hook. Fat Mama could've marched me home to my grandmama and told her what we'd been doing. She could have even called the police. Instead, she gave me a job. I was thankful, and I had to admit, I was excited and relieved that I had a real opportunity to make some money to do my part. It was at that moment that I knew Fat Ma would eventually become someone significant in my life. And although she was initially stern, Fat Mama's kindness had me feeling like I'd won the Georgia lottery.

Living with my grandmama had been rough. It was a stark comparison to how we had previously grown up. My mama and daddy weren't rich, but we got what we wanted and always had everything we needed. We kept new clothes and shoes and weren't used to going without. That changed when we got to my grandmama's. We went from more than enough to nearly nothing. She had been poor most of her life and living in deep poverty had become her norm.

My grandmama lived in an ol' country ass town called Beetlesburg. Although it was dusty and country than a mother-fucker, it was definitely still hood. Fights, shootings, robberies, and murders all occurred there. The crime rate was high and the solve rate was low. It was about forty-five minutes from Atlanta. It was a place where most people didn't have or come from much. We were probably the poorest family in the town, but it was rare that folks did anything for us or even offered. Some people whispered about it, while others spoke about it openly. While they talked, no one ever helped. They either didn't have it, or they simply didn't care.

Every now and then, our uncle, Grandmama's estranged son, would stop by and help us out. We barely knew him. We just knew that he was my grandmama's child and mama's brother. Even though he was her own son, my grandmama wouldn't let him in the house, and she would always yell for him to stay away from us. Probably because he was a drunk that smelled like beer and piss. Plus, he seemed to have mental issues. His name was Otis and despite all the bad things about him, at the beginning of every month he would stumble up to the front porch and leave a bag of food.

He'd been doing that for years and even though he wasn't supposed to come there, we welcomed his monthly arrival and even sat in the window and waited for him when the time neared. Everything helped, but we lacked so much that nothing ever seemed to be enough.

"You good?" my big sister Satin asked as soon as I walked into the house we shared with our grandmother.

"Whatchu think?" I grumbled.

"The hell you mad at me for? You know the pact we made," she said through a lowered voice so my grandmama wouldn't hear.

Even though she was sick and didn't say much these days, her ass could still hear very well.

"Who said I was mad?" I asked her, before rolling my eyes.

"Whatever, Cash."

She dismissed me with a wave of her fingers. Clearly, she'd noticed my shitty attitude and was returning the energy. She had been leaning against the sagging kitchen countertop drinking a glass of cloudy water when I walked in. Now she just stared at me with a frown.

I didn't bother responding. I just tossed the items on the aging, yellow, seventies-style kitchen table and plopped my body into one of the rickety chairs. I was mad but she was right; I remembered the pact. We vowed that during our theft runs that we would split up and if one got caught, the other would bail. Despite knowing this, I couldn't help but still be upset. She was my big sister and a part of me felt like she should be the one taking all the risks. That, unfortunately, wasn't the case for the three of us. It couldn't be like that. We were poor as hell, and everybody had to get out and find a way to hold their own weight, even Nook, who was the baby.

Satin and I would walk around stealing shit, while Nook made a few dollars running errands for the corner hustlers. None of it was much, but something was better than nothing. Some of the basic things people took for granted, we lacked. We barely had food, toothpaste, or even toilet paper. We got government assistance, but it was very little because my grandma got a check. Most of that check was used to pay for all the medicine she needed for the month. By the time she got all her prescriptions out of the way, there was barely enough money to buy two weeks' worth of food. We stuck to the core items like meat. We paired everything with rice and my grandmama never wasted money on vegetables. To her it was a luxury that we just couldn't afford.

"You get toilet paper?" I asked Satin. The thick wad of tissue shoved in my panties in place of a pad was soaked in blood and soon wouldn't be able to hold much more. It was disgusting but shit like that, we were simply used to. We did what we had to do.

"Yeah, I managed to swipe one roll. I'm flat broke and Grandmama only had a dollar in her drawer."

She said it shamefully, although it wasn't shit to be ashamed about. Yeah, she was seventeen, but there weren't too many places in Beetlesburg for a teenager to work other than the handful of retail stores, a few fast-food restaurants, and the local movie theater. Needless to say, they were usually fully staffed with mature, grown folk who barely had a lick of education, so places like that weren't eager to hire teens who wouldn't be nearly as reliable. That was the reason most people took off as soon as they became of age, because there wasn't shit for nobody where we lived.

Satin's eyes shifted to the items that I'd tossed on the table.

"Good, you got three cans," she said happily before leaning down to grab all three cans of potted meat off the table.

"That's gotta last a couple days," I warned her before she got greedy and fucked up the little bit of food we had.

"Nah, we're good. We can each get our own can. It's the first of the month so Mr. Otis brought us a bag. I already put it away in the cabinets. This month, he got us stuff that'll last, like peanut butter, Vienna sausages, and tuna fish. Plus, I'm about to head out in a few. I gotta go upstairs and get ready. I got something lined up with Monique and Amber."

"Something like what?"

My brows dipped in curiosity and concern. Anybody that knew Monique and Amber knew that they were bad news. Like Satin, they were only seventeen, but they were always in somebody's business or in somebody's man's face. Just a month ago, Monique fought a grown woman for allegedly sleeping with her husband. She had been going back and forth with the lady for weeks until she caught her coming out of school and beat her ass in front of everybody. And don't get me started with Amber, who ran away from home once a month. From what I'd heard, her daddy was a drunk that beat her mama up at least once a week. I knew the saying 'birds of a feather flocked together,' so I knew Satin was no damn saint.

"Don't worry about it. Just know that I'm out trying to make sure we straight. Grandmama has been sleeping most of the day and if she wakes up, you just make sure she eats something and goes back to sleep. Don't say nothing to her or Nook about me being gone."

I sighed. I couldn't hide my worried expression, but I still nodded my head in agreement.

"Don't worry. I'll be back before you and Nook wake up in the morning."

This wasn't the first time that Satin had left with Monique and Amber, so I wasn't worried at all.

"Okay," I finally said, expecting shit to go as it always did.

Chapter 4
Satin Ellis

"You sure you know how to drive?" I asked Amber from the backseat of her father's old, pissy pickup truck.

"Yeah, girl. I've been driving since I was twelve, and there's no way in hell that I'd be fuckin' with Atlanta traffic if I didn't know how. I wouldn't even take the chance of fuckin' up my pop's shit."

"You ain't ask him to borrow it?" Monique asked, turning her head to the side to eye her from the front passenger seat.

"Yeah, I asked him to take it to the store. He thought I was coming right back and he damn sure don't know that I'm taking it to Atlanta."

Monique shook her head from side to side but didn't say anything. It was just like some shit that she would do, only she had turned it up a notch. I, of course, said nothing. I didn't want to do or say anything that caused her to change her mind.

Just a reminder of the city that awaited us sent an exciting chill through my body. While Amber sped down the dark country road, I couldn't help but stare out the window and feel a little relief. I needed some money and the thought of getting it so easily was all that was on my mind. Atlanta was the city where dreams came true, and I couldn't wait to get there.

Monique's mama had gotten her an iPhone for her birthday and with it, she found us a little private dancing gig online. We'd done one before, but it was a couple towns over, dancing at a birthday party. We knew that Atlanta was the place to be to make some real money. All we'd been hearing for years was how broke, country girls like us went to Atlanta, danced, and made something of themselves. That's all we wanted and needed: a break. A way out of poverty and a way out of the dusty little nothing-ass town that we grew up in. Neither of us had stellar grades nor a special talent, but we were cute, and we knew how to shake our ass. So, with her new phone, Monique posted some updated pictures of us that we'd taken and began searching for something that we could get into and make some money. We all had the looks and the body to hit the city and make some money, and we all knew how to dance just like the girls we saw in the music videos. We just needed a chance. Luckily, that chance would come quicker than we imagined.

Monique had befriended a nigga on social media a couple years back. He was about the same age as us and from the Atlanta area. After seeing her updated pictures, he reached out to us, offering to show us around since he lived in and knew the area. Since we weren't quite eighteen yet, there were only a few places that would let us dance. He would show us those places. I was excited about meeting him. I low-key couldn't wait to meet the person that would play a role in changing my life. It didn't matter how young he was. Just leading us to the money was good enough for me. It was unusual to see. I was eager that he wanted to see us get money as much as we wanted to ourselves. I needed money like yesterday.

My situation was different than my friends. Amber came

from a two-parent household and Monique's mother worked at the local Family Dollar. They struggled but they didn't know poverty like I did. I had never even owned a smart phone, whereas Monique was on her mom's phone plan and was able to get an updated phone every couple of years. My siblings and I rationed food every month and we often went without basic shit like lights and heat. We didn't get shit like soap, hair products, and pads regularly. Just last month I had to rip pages out the phonebook that my sister and I could stuff into our panties because we didn't have pads. Most bitches couldn't walk a mile in my shoes.

When we first moved with my grandmama it was rough. We weren't used to going without. Over time, we had no choice but to adapt. Eight years later, we were older, tired, and we didn't want to live that way anymore.

"How much longer we got 'til we get there?" I asked.

I was tired of sitting in the cramped quarters of that little ass truck. Amber's dad had beer cans piled up on the seat and the ash tray in the back was overflowing with cigarette butts. The truck also reeked of urine. I had a feeling that Amber's daddy had passed out drunk and pissed himself on more than one occasion. I'd mentioned it but, of course, she denied it. But I knew piss when I smelled it.

"'Bout fifteen minutes," Monique finally answered.

Since she was the one with the phone, she was in charge of using it to get us to and from the location.

That fifteen minutes she claimed we had left, ended up actually being a half hour. Since parts of the route were extremely remote, Monique's service was in and out. We ended up taking several wrong turns before we got into Atlanta. When we finally rolled up to our destination, I was a little uncomfortable. I thought we were going to meet him at a small club or some type of establishment, but the address he sent ended up being a private address in a very beat-down, urban residential area of the city. It was a far cry from what I expected.

My eyes scanned up and down the block. There were a couple drug addicts lingering around while trash littered the street. I didn't say anything because I didn't want to sound like I was complaining and wasn't thankful for the opportunity.

"We're here," Monique finally said as Amber pulled her dad's truck against the curb and cut the engine. We were parked in front of a brick rancher that had three guys sitting out front. They weren't what I expected. To put it mildly, they were hood niggas.

"That's Zander," Monique said proudly as she stared at him from the window.

I eyed the side of her face and couldn't help but notice the googly eyes that she was giving him. She was looking at the nigga like she wanted some dick from him. I hoped she didn't intend to mix business with pleasure, because I was there strictly for the money. I was poor; I wasn't stupid. I wasn't trying to let anything come in the way of me getting me and my siblings up out of the situation we were in. I damn sure hadn't rode all the way from Beetlesburg to Atlanta to link up with some niggas for absolutely fuckin' nothing.

"Wassup ladies?" Zander stood up and greeted us after we finally got out the truck, walked across the grass, and approached the porch.

"Hey Zander," Monique smiled flirtatiously. "These are my girls I was telling you about, Amber and Satin."

The two of us let out a nervous hello while the other men with Zander stood up and gawked at us.

"Oh yeah. Y'all gon' make some money for sure," one of the two men said confidently while he continued to eye us up and down.

He was a big, black heavy-set guy with big poppy eyes. He looked like he grunted when he talked and sweated out motor oil. He stared at us intensely, so I averted my gaze. I didn't want that nigga to think for a second that I was even remotely interested in his ass. My eyes landed on the other guy. He was attentive but remained silent.

"Oh, I apologize for being rude," Zander said, looking to his side as his homies. "This my folks. That's Chop," he said, pointing to the fat dude. "And that's Bilal." Bilal acknowledged us with a nod but continued to stand there quietly. With his low-cut Ceasar and handsome features, he would have been attractive if he didn't appear so unfriendly.

"Y'all can come in real quick," Zander insisted, motioning us into the home with the wave of his hand. "I wanna go over a couple things and then in an hour or so, we can slide up to a spot I know out in East Point. I know for sure that nigga will let y'all get up on that pole. Even if he doesn't have you front and center, he got a backroom for y'all to do some private dances in. Either way, there's still money to be made."

"That's what we like to hear," Monique said, clapping her hands together and following Zander into the house. Amber and I trailed closely behind her with Chop and Bilal not far behind.

"Why you ain't got no furniture?" Monique asked as soon as we stepped inside the house.

My eyes scanned the interior and noticed the same. Despite appearing presentable on the outside, the house was nearly empty inside. I mean, there wasn't one single stitch of furniture in sight. The only thing inside of the house was some broken blinds dangling from the window, a few crates to sit on, and a couple half-eaten containers of Chinese food. It looked like a damn trap house. Something didn't feel right, and my gut was screaming for us to get the fuck up out of there. Zander and

Chop took a seat on two of the three crates before Zander replied.

"We ain't got around to that yet," he said.

"Umm ... Monique, I'm not feeling this. I'm out," I declared after a brief moment of thought.

I was one that went off vibes and energy and everything in me was saying this wasn't it.

"Yeah, me too," Amber cosigned nervously.

I backed up a few feet and she began to follow me.

"Ain't nobody finna go nowhere," Zander said.

I looked at him like he'd lost his damn mind. He and his fat ass homeboy were still sitting on the crates, now eyeing us a little more intensely.

"There's been a change of plans though. We gon' still get this money, but I'm gettin' a cut off the top and y'all ain't gon' be dancing."

The way he said the shit, it was like we didn't have a choice.

As soon as I walked in the house and saw the lack of furniture, I had a feeling they were on some bullshit, and his statement just proved that I was right. I nervously glanced at Monique, who was standing still, looking fucking clueless. I wanted to hit that bitch in the mouth. I had a feeling that she had got us in some shit, and I wasn't sure how we were going to get up out of it. I didn't even know what Zander had planned for us, but judging by his tone, I knew that it wasn't pleasant *or* legal. Despite what his ass said, I took another couple of steps in the direction of the door. Wasn't nobody going to tell me that I couldn't leave.

Zander and Chop stood up. I sensed danger and eyed the door again. It was my only path to safety. Bilal, who also happened to be the smaller of the three, was standing by the door that I so desperately wanted to get out of. I figured that if all three of us made the dash to the door at once, then we could get outside and out of that weird ass house. Bilal wasn't that big and if we had to take his ass down, then we could do so collectively. As long as we moved quickly. I was about to take my chances. I just hoped Amber and Monique would follow suit.

"Fuck this!" I muttered before racing toward the door. Amber ran behind me.

Before I could get my fingers on the handle, Bilal struck me directly in the face with a closed fist. My nose opened up and I fell backward into Amber and hit the floor. I threw my hands to my face and held my nose. It was gushing blood and felt broken.

I'd never been hit like that before in my life. My parents handed out ass whippings when I was younger, but they weren't shit. My grandmother never gave us any real beating. She'd smack our ass with a slipper here and there, and I'd never been in a fight. Not even with my sister, so the blow was shocking and unexpected for me. The pain was excruciating and damn near blinding. In response, I began screaming at the top of my lungs.

"What the fuck, Zander!" Monique hollered. Her voice was overflowing with panic.

"Shut that bitch the fuck up!" Zander ordered.

When I turned to look at Zander, he now had out a gun. Bilal had me by the hair and was hovering above me like he wanted to kill me. Chop was up and now standing close by Monique and Amber. His face had hardened, and his expression was almost daring them to run.

It was déjà vu. Thoughts of my parents' murder rushed to my mind, and I almost passed out. Fear and panic washed over me. I felt like I was reliving that shit all over again. Just like that dreadful night, I knew we were in grave danger, and it was going to end horribly. I squeezed my eyes shut in a desperate effort to block out what was happening. It didn't work. A few seconds later, Bilal's strong grip would lift me partially off the floor by the base of my ponytail.

"Getcho ass up, bitch. Try some shit like that again and it's gon' be more than you getting knocked the fuck down," Bilal said, finally speaking for the first time. "You understand?" he asked, tightening his grip.

His voice was gruff, deep, and commanding. Nothing like I expected him to sound like.

I nodded my understanding and then opened my eyes to let the tears fall from them. Bilal still kept a grip on my hair as Zander walked over. He shoved a small, white pill in my face and demanded that I take it.

"Swallow it," he ordered.

I wanted to refuse but I knew that shit would only get worse. So, I instead, did as told and washed it down with the half-drunk bottle of water that he had in his other hand and had shoved in my face, ordering for me to drink. Neither of the two niggas gave a fuck that blood was still running down my face like a damn river.

"Bilal, take those two bitches to the back," Zander commanded, motioning toward Amber and Monique. "And Chop, get this stupid ass bitch something to stop this blood," he said, finally acknowledging the fact that I was damn near about to bleed to death.

Chop nodded while I looked on, my eyes wide with terror while I continued to hold my nose. Blood was everywhere and seeping through the cracks of my fingers.

"Hold ya fuckin' head back," Zander commanded.

I did as I was told, feeling some of the blood slipping to the back of my throat. A few seconds later, Chop returned with a towel that looked like someone had wiped their ass with it. I didn't have a choice but to avoid the shitty-looking stains and use it to apply pressure to my nose to stop the bleeding. Not long after, the pill that Zander had given me started taking effect. I began to feel different. One minute my head was spinning and the next minute I woke up drowsy with Chop on top of me.

If I was sober, I would have thrown the fuck up, but I was high as a kite and floating in the clouds. I had been drugged. I knew what was going on, but there was nothing I could do about it. I couldn't fight and I could barely talk. My words came out slurred. I was powerless and the only thing I could do was lie back and let the fucked-up shit happened. The drugs helped, and in a sense, I was thankful for them.

By sunrise I'd been raped repeatedly. After Chop, I counted three men, and after that, I stopped counting.

Chapter 5
Ezekiel "Wolf" Griffin

Present Day

"Out of all the shit to try and tie me to, this the shit they choose to associate my name with?" I argued. I leaned back in the recliner in my lawyer's office and waited for a response.

"This shit been all over the news, Wolf. They're cracking down on this human trafficking shit and they're coming down on anyone that's supplying them or aiding them in any way. They pulled nearly twenty girls out of that house," he reminded me, as if I hadn't heard him a few minutes ago when he told me.

"Some were as young as twelve and thirteen years old. That's some crazy shit. Imagine being abducted that fucking young and forced to sell pussy. And these aren't just Black girls. Some were White, Hispanic, and Asian."

"I'm sorry to hear that, but that don't got shit to do with me," I said with zero empathy.

Life was fucking tough. I knew that firsthand. And while I wished shit like that didn't happen, it did. That was life.

"Yeah, well, I'm not saying you're under investigation. What I am saying is, your name came up and you need to be careful. Sources say they're your drugs. They're one of a kind, Wolf."

"Yeah, well those sources can suck my fucking dick," I countered, imitating his voice and tone.

"Damn, Wolf. Yo' heart fucked up like that?" he asked, shaking his head in disbelief and giving me a look that indicated that he was disappointed in a nigga's logic.

I didn't give a fuck though. Life was what it was.

"Look nigga, stop looking at me as your cousin for a moment and instead look at me as your lawyer. I'm advising you to stop movement until this case dies down. They may not be able to prove that the drugs came directly from you, but if they grab one of those fuckin' rich-ass white boys up that you insist on supplying, then they're damn sure gonna be able to tie them to you."

"I don't give a fuck what they can tie me to. I only care about what they can prove."

I paused for emphasis and shot my cousin a long, menacing gaze.

"And you and I both know that if I nigga ever speak my name, they won't do too much talking after that."

"As true as that may be, why even take the chance? Cut those crackers off cuz, or pass the fuckin' torch over to someone else."

I sighed and sat in silence for a moment. He was right. I was richer than a motherfucker and only sold drugs to keep a team of young, hungry Black niggas fed. We only sold to already-rich white boys in an attempt to limit the impact it had on our community.

Outside of a bitch-ass nigga named Buster and some pussy-ass Spanish niggas known as the Diego brothers, or DB, I was one of the biggest drug dealers in the A. I also had a shitload of legal money, so my whole team could be flashy and flamboyant in public because I had them all legally on my payroll.

"Pass the torch over for what? That bullshit that they're using to do whatever the fuck it is that they're doing, doesn't have shit to do with me or mine," I continued to argue.

It was true. I didn't sell junkie drugs. I sold shit that produced an overwhelming feeling of nostalgia. Think ecstasy or party drug. There was no way that they could use my drugs for the shit they were doing. They were drugging bitches so that they were incapacitated.

"You're not here to argue, you're here for counsel," Kwame reminded me. "And as your counsel, the advice I have for you is to relax for a few weeks. They're going to be sweeping the city for these brothels and you know those motherfuckers will take down any and everybody to appease the public."

"Yeah, whatever," I mumbled before standing up from the leather chair I had been seated in.

"I'm serious, Wolf."

I glared at him so he could stop talking. I didn't want to hear that shit. I was twenty-three years old and I wasn't passing over shit until I got good and ready. My family had a habit of repeating shit to me when they felt I wasn't going to listen. That way they could say they tried.

Kwame was my older cousin. He had me by about five or six years. He'd graduated at the top of his class and had been practicing law for a few years. He was a damn good lawyer and because he was my cousin, I trusted him. A little bit anyway. He was a smart nigga with connections I had no idea he'd even formed. Fucking with Kwame, I'd been introduced to other high-powered attorneys, several members of the city council, and even then it was good in many ways but bad in others. Family or not, I didn't want a nigga knowing too much about me, nor telling me what I should and shouldn't be doing.

"I heard you, nigga," I finally replied, breaking my rock-hard gaze.

Kwame sighed and locked his fingers together before bringing them up to his lips. While I walked toward the door, he remained seated at his desk and stared at me. The creases in his forehead revealed his frustration. I was a pain in his ass, just like he was a pain in mine. Mostly because I did my own thing and was highly selective on the advice that I took. Outside of kiddie jail, I'd never been in trouble, so I never understood why he was always on my back. Plus, I was so fuckin' rich that I was nearly untouchable. It was his job to ensure the rest.

"Why don't you go visit Fat Ma," he suggested, as if a light-bulb went off. "She's been asking about you and says she hasn't seen you in a while."

"Ain't nobody trying to go back to that shitty ass town."

I rejected that idea quickly. Wasn't shit in Beetlesburg for a nigga to see or do. No entertainment and no bitches. The ones they had were poor, dusty, and didn't want shit but to mooch off a nigga.

"You got the fuck up out of there as soon as you could, just like I did," I reminded him sternly, now hanging on the door-knob of his office, ready to exit.

Kwame was also from Beetlesburg. Our fathers were actually brothers. I couldn't stand that nigga's daddy just like I couldn't stand my own. And just like our fathers, we were like night and day. Don't get me wrong, we were both smart as fuck. Much more intelligent than the average Black boy. But while I chose a dark path, Kwame chose a bright one. He excelled in school and got a full ride to Morehouse. He was now one of the hottest up-and-coming defense attorneys in Atlanta. I went to prison, did some illegal shit, and just happened to get rich from it.

"I'm serious, Wolf. Go relax. You're damn near thirty."

"Nigga, I ain't no fuckin' thirty. You thinking about yo' own old ass."

"I said *damn near*," he laughed, but it wasn't funny to me.

His ass had added damn near a decade on a nigga.

"Well, trust me, it goes by fast and before you know it, thirty been done crept up on you."

"Whatever," I grumbled, waving him off.

"Seriously cuz. Go relax for a little. Go see Fat Ma, go fuck some honeys."

I looked at Kwame and then started to laugh. We didn't call bitches that anymore. But of course, his ass wouldn't know because he was gay. Had been that way all his life. And although our family never judged him for it, the people in Beetlesburg did. He always said he would move to Atlanta because it was a place where there were more people like him, and he could be free.

"All jokes aside, I hear you," I finally told him once I stopped laughing. "I'll chill for a little while. I'm not staying up that bitch long though. The most I got for Fat Ma is one week, unless she wanna bring her ass back with me. Once my week in hell is over, I'll stop back by and then we can touch base on how shit looking."

"Sounds like a plan," Kwame told me before I left.

"Just make sure you let them niggas know to keep my name out they fuckin' mouth," I said before opening the door and heading out.

* * *

The saying was 'monsters weren't born but created.' I believed it because I was a prime example. I became less of a man when I lost my mom and sister just a few days apart, but when I moved to Atlanta, it was then that I became a monster. There was no other way to be in a city as ruthless as the A. Even to this day you always had to be on point and watching your back to keep a motherfucker from coming up off you. People were always scheming for ways to come up. They would scam, rob, steal, and finesse you out of whatever they could. Genuine people were rare and if you weren't careful, you'd find yourself on one end of the gun. You'd end up with your life taken or taking someone else's.

Personally, I'd killed a lot of people. Motherfuckers didn't get the chance to play with me. All I needed was for a person to look like they were about to, or sound like they were about to, and I'd cut their water straight off. If a person crossed me, they were dead, and if they posed a threat to me, they were dead. I didn't give a fuck if two days had passed, or ten years.

I'd learned early in life to protect your body and loved ones at all costs. I also learned to protect my heart. The niggas you loved would cross you, and they'd get deal with as if I hadn't known them a single fucking day of my life.

I went to a boot camp when I was fourteen. Just a little over a year after my mama died. To be completely honest, I was angry and lashing out at everyone. Mainly my father. I blamed him for her death, and even though he, too, claimed he blamed himself, his words weren't good enough for me. He got to mask his pain while I was forced to deal with mine. There was no alcohol numbing me. Nothing to help me forget for a little while. It wasn't fair that I was forced to live with the trauma he caused while he felt good for a while. Nah, I made sure he felt pain just like I did.

I'd always been big and strong for my age and at fourteen, I stood eye to eye with my father. Seeing him walking around drunk and seemingly at peace sent me into a rage. There wasn't a day that went by that I didn't try to beat his ass to death. My father had felt every knuckle on both my hands plus the power of their grip, because several times I'd choked him until he passed out. He never fought back. He just took it. Every punch I threw, he'd just curl up and cry like a baby. A big ass coward. I'd usually laugh at niggas who responded to beatings like that, but I didn't when it came to him. I pitied him.

Every day that passed, I respected him less and less. The nigga was walking around drunk when the people responsible for his wife's death were walking around untouched. For that, I'd beat him. I'd beat him until Fat Ma screamed for me to stop. Most times, she'd have to intervene with slaps and punches to the back of my head. I mean, after all, he was her flesh and blood. It got so bad that she kept us apart because she swore that I was going to wind up killing him. She knew nothing would give me more pleasure. She converted her basement for a private space for him and kept it locked. She knew as long as he was out of sight, he would be out of mind. She was right, but that didn't take away the anger I felt.

With Fat Ma protecting her bitch-ass son like a hawk and me no longer being able to unleash my frustrations upon him, I started taking it out on any of the kids at the school. I didn't bother the females; it was the niggas that I started beating and banging on. Said something slick, looked at me wrong, or even used the wrong tone, and I was on one. I'd let a nigga talk shit and then sit quietly for a few minutes while I untied my shoe, just to strangle his ass with it. I was a bully. Picking fights and starting shit just because I needed to wail on a nigga. I had also become extremely violent. One time, I bit down on a nigga's nose after dropping him and hopping on top to beat his brains in. I don't know what made me do it. I just did. Tried to rip that bitch off his face. Of course, I stopped doing shit like that when I realized I could catch some shit.

For the school, the final straw was when I folded one of those white motherfuckers up. A teacher. He called himself talking shit until I broke his jaw and then dragged him to the bathroom and pushed his head into the toilet so he could feel like he was drowning. I'd never been more satisfied in my life. The shit was still funny to this day. That's when the police and courts actually sent my ass away. That, of course, ain't stop nothing.

When I left Beetlesburg, niggas knew that I wasn't the one to be fucked with. I wanted to get that through everybody's head since my pops surely wasn't letting folks know.

They sent me to boot camp, but nothing changed while I was there either. I became even more violent, only it was aimed at niggas who actually thought they were tough. I had become evil. When people provoked me, I wanted them to feel pain similar to what I had bottled up inside.

I was quiet and always in thought, but everybody knew those thoughts were violent ones. The sooner they learned that the better. After a while, people said I was crazy and left me alone. Unless they wanted to cop something I had, everyone stayed away. Everyone except a man that would eventually become my best friend.

I met Senator in boot camp. He was what niggas considered crazy too, but he was a different type of crazy. While my thoughts were dark and twisted, Sin was passionate and impulsive. Most of his fights stemmed from arguments. He was charismatic, likable, and loyal to a fault if he fucked with you. The day they brought him in, they stuck him on the bunk above me. We were in a dorm-like setting and out of all the people to befriend, he chose me. Even after I snubbed him, he was persistent about becoming friends. He never said it, he just kept talking to me and asking me questions. He'd try to find ways to make me laugh and even make it his priority to wait for me and walk with me to every meal. We were just sixteen at the time. After a while, the nigga just grew on me.

Eventually, Sin was the one that had a nigga laughing again. That had a nigga hopeful again. It was because of him that I knew that blood didn't make you family. We grew thick as thieves, maxing out of the system a few months apart. He left first because he was a little older than I was, but being the loyal motherfucker he was, he was there waiting for a nigga at the bus stop when I touched down. I remember him looking all over for me with a bag of clothes and a pair of shoes. He'd brought his cousin Cheese along for the ride and they took me to get a meal and a haircut. I remember feeling relieved when he told me that he had a place for me to stay. We would be staying at a small crib in the hood that Cheese had. Sin was the realest nigga I knew, and I had no doubt that he would be my homie for life.

When I met Senator, I decided that I wasn't going back to Beetlesburg. I was heading to Atlanta. I was free from the shackles of the juvenile system, but I knew I had a long way to go before I was free from the shackles of my childhood trauma. I couldn't fuck with Beetlesburg until I accomplished a few things. I had a plan to get money and I also had a plan to commit a whole lot of murders.

I wanted revenge against the niggas that had robbed me of my family. Despite knowing that revenge would only make me feel better temporarily, I was okay with settling for that. I would take that over nothing.

Buster.

According to my father, Buster had ordered his goons to come into our house looking for him the night of the home invasion. He was primarily responsible for destroying my family and I wanted him dead. Fat Ma would never forgive me if I killed my father, but wasn't nothing or nobody stopping me from getting at everyone else involved.

The day I stepped off that Greyhound bus and onto Atlanta asphalt, I went from a piece of a man to a stone-cold killer. Anyone that ever did me wrong would be hunted and anyone who ever played with me in the future would be tortured. My name wasn't just Wolf. *I was a wolf,* and so were any niggas I ran with.

* * *

After arranging to meet up with Sin later that night to handle some business, I headed over to see my left-hand, Tara. Tara's husband, Cheese, held that very same title until the nigga ended up missing about six months ago after a business trip to Tennessee. Just like his cousin Senator, Cheese was a playboy that could have made a lot more money if he made smarter moves and wasn't too busy chasing and getting caught up with bitches. His trip to Tennessee wasn't well thought out and was an attempt to expand. An attempt that I tried to discourage because it wasn't necessary. He was a boss though and nobody could tell him shit.

Tara knew everything about the business because Cheese had taught her. It wasn't unusual for him to bring her with him whenever he did business. For those reasons, we still confided in her when it came to business. With minimal education and being a stay-at-home mom, she wanted to feel a part of something, so we allowed it after Cheese left. It kept her slightly occupied and it kept some money in her pocket. Money she really didn't need since Sin and I made sure that she and the kids had everything they needed.

"Uncle Wolf!" Tara and Cheese's children greeted me as soon as I walked into the house.

Tara lived in a high-rise in downtown Atlanta. It was one of those buildings where a nigga had to be buzzed up and security was on site.

"Heyyyy!" I replied, smiling brightly as I dropped down on one knee and opened my arms to welcome their hugs.

Tara had three children by Cheese. Two boys and one bad ass girl that probably should have been a boy. Amir, Amar, and Amya. With her pink dresses and boboes in her hair, one would've thought Amya was an angel, but looks definitely were deceiving. Shit, I'd come close to whooping her little ass my damn self. A few years back when she was a toddler and sunk her damn teeth into my arms, and about a month ago when she and the boys were fighting, and she threw something that sideswiped my head. She was lucky that I loved her and she was too cute to wail on.

"Hey Wolf!" Tara greeted me as she walked out into the living room from the back of the condo looking like the cleaning lady instead of the girlfriend of a drug-dealing millionaire.

Tara was a pretty girl with smooth, butter pecan skin. Small in stature, sweet, and rocking a pixie-cut, she reminded me of a young Jada Pinkett back in her *A Different World* days. People always said she looked like her.

"Wassup, girl," I replied before walking into the dining room and taking a seat at her glass table.

Dropping in on Tara and the kids was my weekly routine. To be honest, Cheese and I were so close that I loved his family like they were blood. I wouldn't even feel right if I didn't step in some kind of way and make them a priority.

"Any news?" she asked.

I never understood why she did that to herself. Cheese had been gone nearly a year and statistically, after being missing that long, the chances of ever being found were nearly zero. Despite those grim statistics, Tara continued to remain hopeful.

"Nah."

I paused for a moment because I was always unsure of what to say after she asked.

"You need anything?" I asked.

I knew she didn't, but I still asked. I knew Cheese had a lot of money when he was around, but I wasn't sure how he had his accounts set up. Tara was on a few, while his mama was on the rest. Just to make sure she and the kids were straight, Sin and I dropped her off money every month religiously. So much, that she was probably swimming in cash. Her condo was paid for, property taxes and HOA fees were paid up, and the kids' tuition was taken care of. The Wolf Pack took care of their own.

"I'm good. You and Sin bring me more than I know what to do with."

She laughed as she picked up a few toys out the middle of the living room and headed toward the kitchen.

"You want anything to eat?" she asked.

"Nah, I'm straight. But you could use a little break and I'm sure the kids wouldn't mind getting out, so throw something on and we'll go out somewhere."

That was the type of shit we liked to do too. Tara had become a hermit since Cheese had gone. She stayed cooped up in the house, trying to stay busy by cooking and cleaning.

"We leaving?" Amar asked from the living room.

"Yeah, if you guys wanna go have some fun. We can go to Urban Air. Go have dinner after?"

I'd intentionally asked the kids so she wouldn't be able to say no. She was clearly depressed, but she wouldn't deny them. Especially if they had their hopes set on something.

"Yay!!!!" all the kids yelled in unison.

I shot an innocent smile to Tara, and eventually her somber expression changed to a smile.

"You think you slick. Let me get them ready."

"Make sure you get yourself ready too. Don't bring yo' ass out here in no dirty sweatpants and a stained shirt," I joked.

She gave me the finger and then walked off with the kids in tow.

Chapter 6
Senator "Sin" Jones

The fragrant aroma of bacon, eggs, and biscuits wafted through the air of my high-rise condo. Just a minute ago I was in a good mood with my mouth watering, ready to eat. But that changed when I checked my drawer, and I had a stack missing out of it. I kept a lot of money in my house so a motherfucker probably thought I wouldn't notice, but I had. And now the bitch had ten seconds to come up off my bread or I was going to mop the kitchen floor with her ass. Straight Ike Turner that hoe.

"The food's almost ready, baby," Lasia said through an innocent smile.

If I didn't know any better, I would have second-guessed myself. Wasn't no way a bitch that fine could be a thief. She looked like an angel. Long, curly hair that she kept piled at the top of her hair all messy. Smooth, creamy skin the color of coffee with a few drops of milk. She was beautiful but I wasn't a dumb nigga, and I knew that the pretty hoes were the most scandalous ones.

"Bitch, fuck that food," I snapped as I walked into the

kitchen and smacked the bowl holding the eggs onto the floor. "You got ten seconds to go get my shit."

"What are you talking about?" she asked.

Her eyes had widened, and she was shaking. I admit that I had quite a temper, but I hated for motherfuckers to play with me. Disrespect always caused me to step out of character. Real quick.

"My fucking money. I know how much I got down to the fuckin' penny. I had one amount last night and now I'm a grand short. That means, you took it. So, bitch, go find my money or you gon' be on the floor with them eggs."

Lasia looked to the floor and then back at me with embarrassment on her face.

"Fuck you look ashamed for? Go get my fucking money!" I screamed, leaning toward her face so I was loud and clear.

I tried to keep my hands off of females, but her ass was asking to be sent headfirst across the room.

"I'm sorry, Sin," she said, tears welling up in her eyes.

I didn't respond. I just watched her walk off and retrieve her purse from wherever she had hidden it. She returned a minute later with all ten one-hundred-dollar bills that she had swiped.

She handed them to me, and I snatched them out of her hands.

"Cruddy bitch. Get the fuck out."

I didn't wait for her to start moving. I grabbed a fistful of her hair and began shoving her ass to the door. She was barefoot and had on just a bra and panties, but she didn't dare ask for her things. She knew she was lucky that I was letting her skate off that easy.

After shoving her out the door, I threw her purse out with her and slammed the door in her face.

The hoes in Atlanta weren't worth a damn. I was twenty-four years old and would have liked to settle down, but I couldn't find a bitch that was worth a fuckin' swallow. They stole, lied, and did cruddy ass shit. The hoes were so money hungry that they'd cheat on a nigga that they fucked with the long way. I had one that damn near stalked a nigga but come to find out, was still letting a nigga that was damn near sixty years old fuck, because he, too, had a big bag.

Bitches literally wanted to do nothing but fuck, get taken care of, and treated like they were princesses. Fuck that. Now I had to admit that I wasn't the most generous of niggas, but I still looked out. A bitch had to have something going for herself or at least give a nigga something that he was lacking. I was always looking over my shoulder, so a broad could at least offer some peace or something. Be a motherfucker's voice of reason. Pussy and a pretty face weren't going to cut it. For some reason, that's all I fucking attracted. Pretty, trifling-ass hoes.

I was a wild nigga that liked to have fun and the bitches I was compatible with and that seemed compatible with a nigga, weren't shit. Fun ass freaks. That's all they were good for. Some fun, pussy, and a good dick suck.

Shaking off thoughts of Lasia, I walked back into the kitchen.

"Damn," I muttered.

I was now actually giving a fuck about that breakfast I had fucked up. Eggs were scattered all over the kitchen floor and the biscuits that were in the oven smelled like they were beginning to burn. I turned the oven off, took the biscuits out, and then grabbed a strip of bacon from the counter. I was going to Door Dash some shit and then hop in the shower so I could get my day started. I'd get a different bitch to clean that shit off the floor later.

* * *

What I tell you about having any and everybody at your crib?" Wolf lectured.

"I knowwww," I said, drawn out and forcefully.

I was irritated and I didn't want to hear him argue for the next twenty minutes.

"Clearly, you don't. You barely knew that bitch but she know your addy. And you put her out naked."

He looked at me in disbelief, even though, through the frown, I could see a smile tugging at the corners of his lips. Deep down, he knew the shit was kind of funny.

"She wasn't naked," I countered. "She had on a bra and panties."

"Nigga, that is basically naked. The point I'm trying to make is what if somebody come looking for you behind that shit? You didn't even let the bitch take her phone."

"She had her purse," I countered.

"Yeah, but no phone to call a ride."

"Front desk could have called a cab for her. She should have thought about a damn phone when she was going through my shit."

"Yeah, well a cab is definitely what you better hope she got in. Because if I was a bitch and didn't have a phone in a situation like that, the first thing I'm gonna do is call a number I know by heart, and that's usually family. A mom, sister, friend. And what's the first thing they gon' do when a bitch been wronged by a nigga?" he asked.

When I didn't answer, he replied.

"Call a nigga to check him."

"You thinking too hard, Wolf."

I waved him off, hoping that would shut him the fuck up, but of course, it didn't. Wolf always had some shit to say and a point to prove. The nigga got on my nerves at times, but he was like my brother. While I was reckless and didn't give a fuck, this nigga was always on some strategic gangster shit. I didn't understand it because Wolf would lay niggas down like it was nothing. I didn't understand why he was making a big deal out of it. If a nigga came for me then he would get smoked.

"And you not thinking hard enough."

"I ain't worried 'bout that bitch or no daddy, brother, uncle, cousin, *or* fuckin' nephew she might have."

Wolf laughed.

"That just goes to show that you don't really know the bitch like you say you do. You should know if there's a nigga ready to step behind her if you do her dirty. I'm done, nigga. Just stay on point."

"I ain't worried 'bout no nigga with clout, let alone no ol' regular ass nigga.

"Like I said, stay on point," he said again.

"Wassup with you?" I asked. "This ain't like you to be worrying about no shit like that. You enjoy laying these niggas down."

"Yeah, only if they did something to provoke the wolf. Not the other way around."

I shrugged. "Life ain't always perfect and sometimes it just might be yo' patna that give a nigga a reason to want to kill us and not the other way around."

Wolf looked at me somberly for a minute and then began shaking his head as a smile crept up on his face. He knew I wasn't wrapped too tight, and although a nigga usually had to do something to make Wolf hunt them down, sometimes I got shit going that caused bodies to drop. And it normally stemmed from bitches.

After ending that conversation, Wolf and I continued to ride in the car, eventually conversing about the other shit we had going on. For the most part, things were going well, although there was some tension among our crew, The Wolf Pack, because of the fact that Cheese was missing and we had no answers.

Just like me and Wolf, Cheese was a head honcho. We sold drugs and distributed among three crews for organizational purposes. Each of us had about five niggas underneath us that delivered our product through the city of Atlanta. Cheese wanted to expand to Memphis and Birmingham, but Wolf didn't approve. We didn't know shit about Birmingham and Wolf didn't feel Memphis was safe enough nor had the upscale clientele we catered to. Both Cheese and I had visited both cities with Wolf on several occasions since he had a shorty out there. However, he wanted to solely focus on Atlanta, saying that being greedy never ended well. Of course, Cheese didn't listen. Being as though we were all partners, he felt that he didn't need Wolf's blessing to expand, so he started making trips to Birmingham and Memphis alone. According to him, he had a couple potential clients or distributors that owned nightclubs in the two cities. A couple business trips in, and Cheese never returned. Calls and texts would go unanswered and eventually became undelivered. No car. No body. Communication completely stopped.

Wolf and I would go down a few times asking questions, but no one knew shit. They'd never met Cheese and the niggas that had met and interacted with him before had done so through Wolf. So, either Cheese was lying to us or niggas were putting on a good front about what had happened to him. We didn't have shit to go off of, and while the shit hurt my heart because he was my blood cousin, I couldn't help but feel angry because all he had to do was listen.

The shit was senseless, and Cheese's disappearance

changed a lot for us. Moving forward, Wolf and I were still partners and complete equals in business, even though he now called most of the plays because he was a thinker and me, not so much. My brain didn't work like that. I was a hyper nigga and wasn't for sitting around getting lost in my thoughts. I acted quicker and went off my gut. So far, it had worked for me.

Wolf was my best friend but personality-wise we were opposites, but when it came down to how we got money and stepped on niggas, we were alike in more ways than one. Both of us would lay some shit down, Wolf's methods were just a bit more dark, twisted, and sinister.

Just like Wolf, I was a getting-money ass nigga. A hustler that was usually the first one up and last one to sleep. I was born poor as fuck in a little town in Tennessee. When I was about three or four, my mama relocated with me and my two sisters to Atlanta. The move didn't change shit. We were still poor as a motherfucker, it was just more people around and more resources available to ease the feeling of being poor. Shit like public housing and food stamps.

By the time I was thirteen, I started hustling. Other kids my age were doing it, even the bitches. After a couple days, I realized I was actually good at the shit. It wasn't enough to move us out the hood or no shit like that, but it was enough to stay dressed to impress and juggle a couple hoes. It was in my sophomore year that I was reminded I still was a poor-ass nigga. I was on a fine ass bitch that was a grade beneath me. She was from the hood too, so it wasn't hard to impress her with a few gifts, meals, and hair from the beauty store. A nigga leveled her up a notch and helped solidify her as one of the baddest in the hood. We were only fourteen and fifteen, but you grew up fast in the hood. We were running around Zone Six as one of the hottest couples. Unfortunately, the attention went to her head, and she started stepping out on a nigga with a hustler selling drugs on a level that I couldn't even imagine at the time. By that time, I was gone over the bitch.

Imagine being fifteen and gettin' yo' dick ate up so good that all you could think about was the way that mouth felt when you were out on the block. I was damn near hustling just to make sure I could keep her laced. She not only cheated, but she took off with the nigga too. That shit hurt a nigga. That same hurt was what forced me to go harder, but I was dumb and the way I was moving landed me in jail and eventually boot camp.

I knew when I got home that I wanted to be at the top of the food chain. I wanted to be at a level so high that there weren't too many above me. That wouldn't have happened if I hadn't met Wolf. At first, my thoughts were on getting rich off coke or boy, but that nigga was so fucking smart that he created an entirely different wave. With his brains and our joint dedication, the moves we made would propel niggas to the top. Of course, we took some losses along the way. Some minor and some devastating. But all of it, making us the men we were today.

"You too eager to settle down."

I rolled my eyes. I wasn't sure what the fuck made the nigga say that. We were talking about business shit, but then again, I was only half listening. Yet, I still responded.

"And you're not eager enough," I countered. "Nigga, we both getting older. I want to come home to a family. A home-cooked meal. Not no takeout. I don't want to have to keep recounting my money to see if a bitch stealing from me. Weighing out packages to see if a hoe stealing my shit."

"Y'all niggas keep saying that we getting old shit."

I wasn't sure who the fuck *y'all* were, but we were.

"We is. And I don't know about you, but I want to be loved,

nigga. I don't wanna keep dealing with no bitches that I gotta watch."

"Well then don't. Stop fucking any and everything so you won't have to. I ain't searching for shit. What's for me will find me."

"Shorty fucked you up in the head. You still human. I know yo' dick still get hard from time to time."

Wolf paused and I knew I had struck a nerve. My patna had always been a dark-ass nigga. He showed his love by buying bitches shit and spending time with them but for some women, it wasn't enough. His ex, Blanca, a bad-ass mixed bitch, wasn't feeling his dark ways. Wolf was dealing with trauma and wasn't eager to address it. To put it simply, the nigga was borderline mean at times. His walls were always up, and you damn near had to scale the bitch to get over it. Blanca was spoiled and wasn't used to the world not revolving around her. But Wolf knew that and still pursued her relentlessly. Shorty got tired of the dreams he was selling and took off on his ass.

"Fuck a hard dick," he finally responded. "It's called self-control. Something you seem to lack."

"Remind me why we're talking about this again?" I asked him.

He didn't respond so I let the conversation end there. Hopefully he wouldn't bring it up again when his weird, Einstein, ADHD brain told him to. Besides, I was done arguing with a nigga that sat around, fake smiling with blue balls. He was the last black-ass nigga I was about to take advice from.

"You talk to them white motherfuckers about that trafficking shit that's been all over the news?" I asked. I was hoping that he had been researching them niggas like he researched me.

"Yeah. None of them claim to know shit, and all of them

denying redistributing our shit to street-level or mid-level dealers," Wolf responded.

I was asking about the high-profile drug trafficking case that had dominated the headlines. We had never delved into who Rick or the others were peddling drugs to because, honestly, we didn't care. We just assumed that they were distributing the work they purchased in their businesses and if they resold anything, it was to other white motherfuckers similar to them.

Neither Wolf nor I wanted our names associated with such a vile enterprise—supplying sex traffickers. We couldn't endorse that. The idea of drugging and coercing young girls into prostitution was beneath niggas. We'd have a bitch in the field trapping before we had one out in the streets selling her ass.

"One of those motherfuckers knows something," I countered, casting a sharp side-eye at Wolf.

I never cared for Rick. I didn't like the way he looked down on people like us. The few times I'd met him, he always had an aura about him, as if he were better. As if he were doing us a favor by taking our drugs. A rich, white motherfucker who owned nightclubs stretching from Atlanta to Miami—that's what he was. Just from his business alone, we pulled in millions of dollars. Palm-colored people loved snorting shit up they nose and popping pills. They'd spend whatever on it and we had no problems taking their money.

Selling to the white boys was Wolf's idea. He believed it was better to poison their communities instead of our own. So far, it had proven successful. The white boys were easy to control, and we never had to worry about engaging in wars or any other violent confrontations because none of them were about that life. Aside from Rick, we worked with three other individuals: Peter, who owned a couple of upscale lounges; Landon, the proprietor of nearly a dozen fitness centers; and

Daniel, another nightclub owner. All of their locations were in the Atlanta and surrounding area.

Our advantage was that the shit we sold could be used for different purposes and served different clientele. In the world of nightlife, everyone knew that the hottest clubs were the ones where the good shit was at. White folks loved their drugs and would pay top dollar for them. And in the fitness realm, the most sought-after gyms were the ones that promised the greatest gains and the most attractive physiques. The drug that we sold was distributed in bulk with two different milligram options. Fifteen milligrams for those using the drug to strength train or have more energy. The affects were similar to steroids except our drug produced a nostalgic high. Distros like Landon would get that dose for his gym. He would also receive a weekly shipment of protein powder through our front company posing as a beverage supplier. Our other distros who owned nightclubs would get the drug in a 30 mg dose, which produced a more intense, euphoric feeling that left people with energy for hours on end. They would also get a shipment of margarita mix to legitimize the transactions. It was a win-win situation for us, and every nigga on our team was paid. Even down to our young boys.

"That's where we're headed to now," Wolf finally said, pulling me from my thoughts. "We gon' roll up in every one of those locations and see if we peep some shady shit."

"Every one?" I frowned. "How we gon' do that? Between the lounges, clubs, and gyms, it's gotta be over a couple dozen spots."

"Yeah, it's gonna take us some time, but we'll get it done. We gon' swing by one of Peter's spots now in Alpharetta. I gave Royce and Butter a list of some other ones to hit, that way we won't be going into the same ones. They're gonna start at night, while we gon' start now."

I glanced at the clock. It was nearly noon. Wolf had picked me up about a half hour after I kicked shawty out. My intention was to get something to eat, but my plans had been changed when I chose to ride out with Wolf instead of driving my own shit. I was hungry as fuck and he wanted to work.

"Man, you gon' have to stop and get something to eat. My mafuckin' stomach growling."

I rubbed my stomach just to show him how real shit was. If he listened closely, he could hear the bitch growling.

"If you hadn't slapped yo' breakfast on the floor, you wouldn't be hungry, nigga."

I laughed.

"Nah, we can stop. Where you wanna go?" he asked.

We were in Buckhead since that's where my condo was.

"That little breakfast spot on Roswell Road. I go in there a lot and they always on point."

"Yeah, I been there a couple times myself."

Since we were already on 19, headed north, Wolf didn't have to reroute.

My thoughts drifted to the chicken and waffles I planned to get when I got there. As we idled at a red light, Wolf turned the volume up on the stereo and began sifting through his playlist. While he played around with that, a burgundy Dodge Durango truck pulled up next to us. The loud rumble of its engine filled the air, drawing my attention. The whip was heavily tinted. My gut churned, sensing danger in the air like a predator on the hunt.

Before I could think another thought, the truck's doors swung open, and two men emerged, brandishing machine guns. Their faces were hidden behind ski masks, but that didn't stop our eyes from locking with one another. They weren't there to chit chat with niggas. Panic surged through my veins as they sprayed bullets in our direction, shattering glass and tearing through metal. Instinct kicked in, and when Wolf slammed his foot on the accelerator, the Escalade he was driving lurching forward.

We were strapped, but it was no need to reach for our guns. They'd caught us slipping and were on our ass. The only thing we could do was duck down as we peeled off, to keep from being shot.

"Go, nigga!" I yelled out, as if that wasn't what he was already trying to do.

Bullets whizzed, glass shattered, and shards fell as the two pussies flexed on us with their machine guns. The air was thick with the bitter scent of gunpowder as we weaved through traffic, barely avoiding death with each passing second. I looked over at Wolf, his reflection mirroring my own as he attempted to duck and drive at the same time.

The escape was a blur, an adrenaline-fueled blur of screeching tires and desperate maneuvers. It felt like an eternity, but we finally managed to put some distance between us and the niggas blasting at us. Eventually the streets, their weapons, and their car faded into a blur as we put distance between us and them.

"The fuck!" I yelled out, my adrenaline rushing.

The chaos had subsided, so I stole a glance at Wolf. His voice was silent, but I could hear him breathing. It wasn't labored but it wasn't normal either. When I looked at him, I noticed blood staining the side of his t-shirt. He was pressing his hand against his side in an attempt to apply pressure.

"Shit! You've been hit!" I yelled. I turned around and looked out the back, my eyes searching for the niggas that were long gone. Wolf's truck was riddled with bullets and all the windows had been shot out.

"Pull over, nigga! Let me drive. I gotta get you to the hospital!" I demanded.

Wolf didn't say anything. He growled quietly in pain and pulled over.

I noticed anger burning in his eyes and I already knew what time it was. As soon as I got him to the hospital and made sure he was okay, it was on and poppin'.

Chapter 7
Cory "Buster" Collins

I sat quietly as my entire crew of fifty plus men looked at me, waiting for direction. Wolf ... Ezekiel "Wolf" Griffin was becoming a fucking thorn in my ass, and it was taking everything out of me not to kill his entire fucking family. I already knew what his issues were with me; however, my team did not. I'd called the meeting to order last minute because things that usually didn't happen, were happening. We were being hunted. My team was completely unaware that the leader of the fuckin' Wolf Pack had a personal vendetta against me because I had initially ordered his father to be murdered because he was a part of a home invasion that had killed my best friend Bobby and his girl Angie.

The Wolf Pack had always been peaceful. They were a team of rich motherfuckers that got money selling a drug that no one else had. For that reason, they were stupid rich and since there was no one to compete with, there was no one that they could be compared to. A couple people had fucked with them and wound-up dead in some real fucked-up ways. Rumors were that the Lopez brothers had tried them, and they also got handled on some guerrilla shit. My crew knew not to fuck with The Wolf Pack because I knew that Wolf could be a real problem if provoked. His trauma probably had him fucked up in so many ways.

I was a powerful man now myself, so I'd done my homework on Ezekiel. I knew his history of violence and I knew that it probably had escalated over the years. Now, he was on one with my team. I wasn't entirely sure why, but I believed it had something to do with him being shot. From what I gathered, it didn't have shit to do with him personally. But now the nigga was hunting down any and everybody he had issues with. That included myself.

Ten years prior, a couple of my men raped his mother and sister. The mom ended up dying from her injuries and his sister killed herself. Chris, E—short for Edward—and Loco were the stupid motherfuckers I'd taken with me that night. I wasn't that smart at the time. The niggas had a history of raping bitches anytime we had to run down on dudes and they were with females. I always turned a blind eye to the shit and let them do whatever because truthfully, I never gave a fuck. Nothing had ever happened because of it. Nobody had ever turned out like Wolf. He was the only nigga that ever had me actually worried. He was powerful enough to have me and my people touched.

Wolf's crew wasn't as large as mine, but they were a lot younger and a lot more vicious. So far, we had been the target of a drive-by that resulted in a triple murder, as well as a Mafia-style double murder. The latter happened at a popular Atlanta eatery and in broad daylight. E and another member of our team were shot in the back of the head while they ate. Altogether, we'd lost five men, and frankly, I anticipated losing a lot more.

"Why we ain't lighting these niggas the fuck up?" Chris asked angrily.

He and E were close. Always had been. He and Loco knew the deep-rooted issues that no one else was privy to.

"We play chess, not checkers. You'll get the green light soon," I told him.

Chris exhaled a frustrated breath and walked off, while Loco just stared at me. I could tell he was angry. His expression was hard and his jaws tight.

"Y'all niggas can go!" I said to my crew.

I waited while they quickly dispersed and then figured I'd give Loco the floor. Clearly, he had something to say.

"You got something to say to me?" I asked him.

"So, we supposed to sit around and wait while this nigga picks off our crew in tiny chunks?" His chest rose and fell, further solidifying his anger.

"That's not what I'm asking," I replied, my expression darkening. "I'm asking you to trust me and let me handle it. If I recall, you niggas are the reason why we in this fuckin' mess."

Loco sucked his teeth before beginning to argue.

"Man, this ain't our fuckin' fault. That nigga bitch-ass pop killed Bobby so we went after him. Ain't nobody know his mom had cancer and that his sister would kill herself. That ain't niggas' fault. He should just be thankful he still got a daddy."

I just stared at him and didn't even bother trying to understand his logic. No matter how they looked at it, it wasn't normal for them to go around raping bitches.

"Like I said before, I'll let you know when it's time to move. Until then, stay out the streets, and stay out of public places. Just stay safe."

Loco didn't bother replying. He spun around on the sole of his Nike's and stormed off.

For men like Wolf, strategy was required. I refused to let their emotions dictate my movement and cause more harm than good.

Chapter 8
Cashmere "Cash" Ellis

"Y*ou have a collect call from ... Nook Ellis. An inmate at the Ware State Prison. If you do not accept this call, hang up. If you accept this call, press zero now."*

I pressed zero and a few seconds later, my brother's deep voice came through the speaker.

"Hello?"

"Hey Nook. How you been, baby boy?" I said joyfully into the phone.

I was genuinely happy to hear from him. It had been a few months since we last spoke and at least a year since I'd seen him. Nook was tucked away in the Georgia prison system in a little town about four hours away.

Three years ago, after I got caught stealing from Fat Mama's store, my whole world changed. The day I would land my very first job would also be the same day that my sister took off with her friends and disappeared off the face of the earth. A month later, Nook was arrested for possession of an ounce of crack cocaine. He was fifteen years old. Come to find out, he was doing more than just running small errands for the drug dealers. He was running packs for them also.

Nook wouldn't snitch and was ultimately charged as an adult and sentenced to four years in prison. Bad behavior like fighting and possessing contraband caused him to max out and serve his entire sentence, but that was nearly done and over with. Nook was scheduled to be released in less than a year, and as much as I hated to see my brother caged up, I would be lying if I said that I was ready for him to come home.

Nook left when he was fifteen, but now at the age of eighteen, he was a completely different man. He had changed so much, and I wasn't sure if any of the changes were for the better.

His conversations were dark and although he tried to sound positive, the negative energy in his voice was there. He talked about getting out and making moves, and while I tried to encourage him to come home and do the right thing, I had a feeling that he had his own plan.

"I'm good, sis!" Nook said happily into the phone.

Our calls were usually short and like clockwork, I knew he was about to ask for something.

"That's good, I'm glad to hear that."

That's how our conversations went. I loved my brother, but the shit was getting old. I was struggling to hold down the shack, because it damn sure wasn't no fort, and every time he called, he was asking me to send him the little bit of money I did have.

"If you got it, can you do something small for me?" he asked.

"Small like what?"

"Can you cash app the same person that you cash app'd last time, like $20?"

Nook lived off the money he made working in the kitchen,

so I didn't put anything on his books. But I would cash app folks from time to time for him.

"Okay, it won't be today, because I'm at work right now, but I'll try to take care of it in a couple days for you."

"Bet. How you been though?"

Nothing had changed on my end, so Nook and I made small talk for a few more minutes until a customer walked in.

"I gotta go, Nook. I'll take care of that for you, but I got a customer and Fat Ma been on my ass about being on the phone," I told him.

"Alright. I'll call you back in a few weeks or something. I love you."

"I love you too."

"You can't just pick shit up and start eating it without even paying for it," I yelled across the store after hanging up the phone with Nook.

My eyes were narrowed as they cut into the fine ass nigga that thought he could just do whatever he wanted to do in Fat Ma's store.

I eyed him intensely as he walked from the aisle he was in and approached the counter where I was standing. I couldn't help but admire his thieving ass. A deep shade of chocolate with eyes that set deep in his face, the man was fuckin' delicious. I was a virgin, but my ass wasn't dead. I could tell he wasn't from around the area. He looked too rich. I wasn't a gold digger, but I would have noticed him or heard about him. He would be somebody in Beetlesburg.

My eyes traveled his frame. His movement was slow ... almost as if he had been injured, but other than that he appeared to be in good physical shape. Like he could have been a football player. His hair was low, tapered on the sides, and spongy looking at the top. His eyebrows even had little lines in them on both sides. He was a city boy and if I had to guess, I'd say Atlanta.

"That's how you treat paying customers?" he asked after reaching the counter.

"Nigga, you ain't paid for shit yet. Please don't open anything up in this store without paying for it first."

People stole all the time but for some reason, he annoyed me more because his wealth was apparent. I'd actually let a few of the kids slide with stealing because I knew they were fucked up like I was. But for someone like him to come in wearing expensive-looking clothes, shoes, and jewelry, I wasn't having it.

"Shawty, yo' attitude is trash. Just ring my shit up."

He reached into his pocket and grabbed the juice and bag of chips that he'd swiped and tossed them on the counter. His face was now turned up like he smelled something rotten. I was about to curse his ass the fuck out for being disrespectful, but I was interrupted.

"Wolf!" Fat Mama squealed out of nowhere.

I looked at her and then back at him. *She knew him?*

"Hey Grandma!" Wolf beamed.

My brows dipped in confusion. Fat Mama ran toward him and threw her arms around him. All I could think about was how fucked I was. My stomach immediately sank to my ass. I had to admit that I was definitely rude to him. Niggas came in the store taking shit, talking shit, and trying to holla at me on the regular. Needless to say, after years of bullshit, I didn't have much patience for any of them when they came. And now it was about to cost me my job. The job that I still desperately needed.

"Why didn't you tell me you were coming?" she asked as she rocked him from side to side.

"Ow, Grandma. Easy now, I'm still healing."

"Oh, I'm sorry, baby. I didn't mean to hurt you. I'm just happy to see you is all."

She released him but still stood there and looked at him with love and admiration. She was genuinely happy to see him.

"It's okay. After I got out of the hospital, I figured I'd come see you before I head out to Florida. Going on a vacation."

"Well, that's good, Wolf. You need it. You need to get away, 'cause lawd knows I couldn't take hearing that you've been hurt again. I've missed you so much," she said tearfully with her voice cracking. She brought her hands to his face and cupped both sides, studying his face proudly. "How are you? You better?" she asked.

"It was a flesh wound so I'm good. Getting my strength back but still a little tender and sore."

He grinned and shrugged. Lawd the man was even finer when he smiled. His teeth were a sparkling shade of white. All except for the front two. They were lined with gold.

Fat Ma gave him a look like he'd better stay out of trouble, and then she turned to me with a beaming smile.

"Cashmere, this is my grandson, Wolf." She looked back at him. "Wolf, this is Cashmere."

A sly grin spread across Wolf's face. "We actually met," he said.

My eyes darted nervously from Wolf to Fat Ma. I just knew he was about to tell her I'd cursed him out, so I parted my lips to plead my case. Before I could say anything, Wolf spoke.

"I'm glad you finally got some decent help up in here. She don't play 'bout niggas stealing," he said with a smile. "Went security mode on me. She cute though, so I didn't mind."

"Yeah, well cute or not, don't you go get no ideas. This girl here is young and pure, and I don't need her young tale getting all distracted. She's one of my best employees. We had a rough start, but I'm thankful she showed up."

Fat Ma stopped gushing about me and turned her attention back to her grandson.

"Come on boy, let's get you back to the house. I haven't seen you in a month of moons. I'll make you something good to eat and then we can play catch up. You can tell me all about what you been up to."

"I'm sure Kwame's big mouth done that already," he chuckled.

She wrapped her big ol' arm around Wolf's and began gently pulling him toward the door.

"Cash, Lou is gonna close up. Straighten up that dairy fridge for me and then you can go on home," Fat Ma instructed.

"Yes ma'am," I countered.

"Bye meanie," he said, flashing me a smile.

"Bye thief," I countered.

As soon as they walked out the door, I let out a sigh of relief. That shit could have ended badly. I made a mental note to watch my mouth and work on my patience. I was barely getting by as it was, the last thing I needed was to lose my job.

Once I finished straightening up the dairy fridge like Fat Ma had asked, I swept up, closed my register, and then headed out. As soon as I walked outside, I found my best friend Israel parked in the lot like clockwork. I smiled as I headed to her beat-up, rusted-red Honda Civic coupe.

"Hey girl," I greeted her.

After my sister went missing, she and I started hanging tight. Israel also happened to be Amber's baby sister. Amber, along with Monique and my sister, had also disappeared. No one had heard from them in two years. There were rumors that they were carjacked and killed but there were never any real leads. It was a true cold case with nothing to go off. No bodies had been found. Their father's truck had never been located. In the end, we accepted the fact that Satin, Amber, and Monique were gone. Stricken with grief and struggling at home, Israel and I started hanging out and formed a bond. It became easier to cope when there was someone that knew the pain you felt.

"Hey frand! How was work?" Israel asked, her long, curly hair blowing wildly from the cool fall breeze that was flowing. Just like Amber, Israel—Izzy for short—was mixed.

She was a thick girl with pale skin and average features. She was actually fairly attractive when she dressed up, which was rare. Like myself, Izzy wasn't big on attention from the deadbeats from the area we grew up in. They usually weren't worth shit, running through and fucking on the same bitches. We didn't want to be a part of that. We just wanted to make some money and eventually get the fuck away from there. Unfortunately, that was easier said than done. We were still human and had blossomed into young women. Even though we didn't want the attention, every now and then someone would catch ours.

"Work was cool," I finally said. "I met Fat Ma's grandson today."

"Who, the gay nigga?"

"Gay?" I eyed her like she was tripping, and then a smile formed on my face. Izzy said anything out her mouth.

"No, he's not gay ... Well, he didn't look like he was gay."

"Nah, the grandson that I've seen is definitely gay and looks gay. What the nigga look like that you saw?"

"He was a hood guy. He looked like he could have been some type of athlete. Fine as fuck with a spongy-looking haircut."

Izzy sat in thought for a few seconds and then shook her head.

"Nah ... I never seen him before."

"Well, I've been working there for two years and have never seen him, so I guess he doesn't come around that often."

"Or maybe you seen him but never paid him any attention because you were too busy worried about Jermaine."

I tore my gaze away from the windshield and cut them at Izzy. The thought of my ex-boyfriend Jermaine made me sick to my stomach. I couldn't stand to hear that nigga's name. He was the poster child for fuck boy.

I met Jermaine about six months back, coming out of the store one night after getting off work. I could humbly admit that I had a smart mouth, but I'd always been quiet for the most part. I ignored the guys in school and when I graduated, I ignored the dope boys just the same. Jermaine, however, was persistent. After a few encounters and some persistence, we started kicking it. At first, things were cool. He would pick me up, feed me, and we even went bowling and to the movies. But at the end of the day, it all came down to Jermaine wanting to fuck. You see, I was the hood virgin. I'd never had a sexual encounter and my hymen was still intact. I'd never even worn a tampon. The sexual encounter part changed when one night at Jermaine's house, he pressured me into letting him eat my pussy. Even though I wasn't ready for all that, I nervously agreed. I couldn't lie, it felt good, but it didn't feel good enough to let him stick his dick in me and take my virginity. Once he pulled his face out my twat and tried to go all the way and realized I wasn't going for it, the nigga went off. Damn near tried to force me. I did the first thing that came to mind; I started swinging and took off out the house.

Jermaine and I were a wrap after that. I didn't want shit to do with him. Blocked him and proceeded to ignore him anytime I saw him out or at the store. Unfortunately, that's when things between me and him went from bad to worse. Jermaine wasn't taking kindly to the rejection and his treatment toward me showed it. Any time I ran into him, he would do some shit to antagonize me. Like come into Fat Ma's store, take a twenty-ounce soda out the fridge, shake it up and then dump it on the floor. Or "accidently" knock over a whole rack of shit. Like I stated before, I had a temper, and I had enough problems, so a bitch's temper was short. After the second incident with Jermaine, I started responding because I knew he was trying to be smart. I told him he was acting like a bitch because I wouldn't give him no pussy. Embarrassed him in front of his little crew. I figured, if he wanted to act like a bitch, I would treat him like one in front of them. Right after, Jermaine stopped getting physical with the items in Fat Ma's store and started trying to get physical with me. He would try to force me to talk to him and when I refused, he would physically assault me to make me. It wasn't unusual for him to yank me to him by my arm, pull me in by my hair and threaten me. Despite him trying to force me to be with him, there was nothing he could say or do to make me continue any type of relationship with his lame ass. His ass was a borderline stalker, even though word on the streets was that he had several bitches to fuck and suck on him. He didn't care about that. He wanted the virgin pussy that had made a mess on his face. At times, I believed it was a pride issue.

Of course, Jermaine was still giving me hell, but thankfully, he didn't know where I lived. I was low-key ashamed of my grandmama's house, so I'd never even allowed him to pick me up in front. I stayed on a long road that had a bunch of ran-down, one-story homes on it. There were a lot of older folks on my block that had been there since my grandma. They sat outside every day because they all collected an old folks check and didn't have shit to do. Jermaine had also never been introduced to my grandma, so he had no idea which one it was even if he did find out the name of the road I lived on. Although we both lived in Beetlesburg, he lived in a different neighborhood, although he still brought his ass over to mine nearly every day.

It had gotten to the point where Jermaine was bothering me so bad that other people would tell him to leave me alone. Some days he would sit outside and wait until I got off. It had gotten so bad that Fat Mama had banned him from the store, even though he didn't comply unless threatened with the police. He wasn't just disrespectful to me; he was also disrespectful to her. I was disgusted and ashamed that I had even held a phone conversation with his ass, let alone allowed him to eat me out. Eventually, after seeing that Jermaine wasn't going to let up, Fat Ma began letting me go a little early. Her other employee, an older guy named Lou, would close up the store. With all that being said, Izzy knew that Jermaine was the last name I wanted to hear her say.

"Girl, fuck that nigga."

The mention of his name caused my eyes to scan the parking lot and surrounding area of the store.

"You haven't seen him, have you?" I asked.

"Nah. When I first started coming out here, I used to, but now, I hardly see him. It's been a few days," she assured me. "I heard he was dealing with some new bitch," she said.

"Good," I mumbled, although I wasn't completely convinced.

I was hoping that the saying was true, 'out of sight, out of mind.' Izzy began heading down the road while I got comfortable in the passenger seat. Before we were a block away, she got a text message. She read it and then immediately deviated from our normal route back to my house.

"Where you going?"

"I gotta meet Damien. He's gonna let me borrow $20 'til next week," she informed me.

Damien was a mutual friend, although he was more hers than mine. He was gay but he kept it on the downlow.

"I would've given it to you." I frowned.

She was my only friend, and she did anything she could for me. It annoyed me that she didn't come to me. Whether I had it or not, she still should have asked.

"I know, but you just gave me money for gas, and I know you trying to hold shit down all by yourself with your grandma sick and all."

At the mention of my grandmama, I got quiet. She was more than just sick; she was dying. Years of unregulated high blood pressure had caused congestive heart failure. She was now in the final stages. Every other week she was in and out of the hospital. She had fluid on her lungs, swollen legs and feet, and a hacking cough that wouldn't go away. My sister was gone and now I had to deal with the fact that my grandmama would be leaving me as well. My life was all kinds of fucked up, but that's how it had been for as long as I could remember.

Chapter 9
Ezekiel "Wolf" Griffin

I leaned against the side of my grandmother's store, running my mouth and people watching. I'd been back in Beetlesburg a few days, kicking it with Fat Ma like Kwame suggested, but I had started to get bored and was ready to head out. The first time I mentioned boredom and rolling out, Fat Ma came up with the idea of having a block party. Something fun that would bring folks out. But I knew it was just to keep me around a little while longer.

As I stood and watched the scores of people gathering out in the field of the community center that Fat Ma had managed to reserve at the last minute, I realized that I barely knew anyone there. A lot had changed since I'd last visited. I hadn't been to Beetlesburg in nearly eight years. After I got out of boot camp, I went to Atlanta and never looked back. I might've slid through once or twice to see Fat Ma, never staying more than a couple of hours. She hated it, but she also realized that it was probably for the best. That's why she was so excited by my arrival this time. It had been so long since she'd spent any time with me.

She'd truly gone out of her way to show me and the community a good time. She'd whipped out several grills and had so much barbecue that a nigga could eat for days. Water slides, bouncy houses, card tables—you name it, it was there. She even allowed niggas to shoot dice on the corner of the store. As long as everyone was peaceful, she didn't care. The shit was so lit that I thought about calling The Wolf Pack to come down; however, I quickly decided against it. I wanted to keep those two families separate.

"What y'all know about shawty over there?" I asked Buck and Johntay after spotting Cash.

They were two niggas that I knew from way back. They were also well-known troublemakers in the town. For the most part, nobody liked either of them, but they'd never done anything for me to dislike them. They were always respectful to Fat Mama, which of course was expected, considering they had actually grown up and went to school with me. Like I said, I rarely visited Beetlesburg, but I'd definitely storm that motherfucker if Fat Ma ever called and gave the word. Luckily, she was respected, and I never had to turn up about her.

"Shawty right there."

I pointed to Cash who was standing in line waiting to get some food with another broad.

"Her. She work up in Fat Ma's. Got a funky ass attitude."

I eyed the young broad. She was average in stature. Borderline petite with nice, shapely hips. Her face was void of makeup and she wore her thick hair up in a bun. She was pretty but her attitude was ugly. Nevertheless, Fat Ma spoke highly of her, and that said a lot. It actually had me curious.

"Oh, Cash. You don't want her, she stiff as fuck," Buck said dryly.

"I never said I wanted her, nigga," I laughed. "But how she stiff?"

"Well, for starters, the bitch got a bad attitude. She cute and all but don't be having no rap for niggas and definitely don't be trying to give that pussy up. I thought she was gay at first, until I heard she was talking to a lame-ass nigga from Blue Creek."

Beetlesburg was small but consisted of a few neighborhoods. Where we were was Oaksdale, and then there Carpenton, and lastly there was Blue Creek. Blue Creek was actually considered one of the better of the three. It was where motherfuckers from Oaksdale or Carpenton moved to if they got a decent job, had some money, and could live a little better. Out of the three, Oaksdale was the worst. It was considered the hood and Fat Ma's was equivalent to the corner store.

"I heard she was a virgin," Johntay finally added.

My brow rose. I was intrigued.

"For real?" I asked.

"Yeah, and I believe it. Bitch be running around like she too good for niggas," Buck said, hopping back in.

"Damn boy, you done called shawty a bitch a couple times now. Why you sound like a bitter nigga?" I laughed. "Did she reject you or some shit?"

"Hell yeah!" Johntay cosigned. "That nigga definitely bitter. He tried to holla at shawty and she wasn't for it. He been talking shit about her since. But before that, when he thought he could get her, he was running around with nothing but positive shit to say."

Johntay began laughing up in Buck's face and I couldn't help but be amused as well. Shawty was a virgin, kept a job, and talked her shit to keep lame-ass niggas like Buck out her face. Sounded like a winner to me, although she definitely needed to adjust that attitude. But then again, I wasn't known for being the nicest nigga myself. Maybe she was just misunderstood or was guarded for some reason. I could only speculate, but I definitely intended to find out more about her.

"Back the fuck up out my face, nigga," Buck demanded, pushing Johntay back a little. Buck was a short, stocky, black motherfucker, while Johntay was a little taller and a lot leaner. I was a pretty good judge of character, and although I'd never seen either of the men fight, all my money was on Johntay. Buck looked like he just talked shit and wasn't about nothing.

"While y'all niggas stand here and go back and forth, I'm gon' see what's up with her. She might not fuck wit' any of y'all niggas around here, but I ain't no regular nigga," I said, ending the conversation with both of them.

I'd heard enough from them. Nobody fucked with shawty because they *couldn't* fuck with shawty. To be honest, I like that shit. I liked the fact that she was exclusive. And if the rumor was true that she was a virgin, that made her top notch in my book. I wanted to see for myself where her head was really at. A bitch could still be a virgin and not about shit.

"So, Cashmere. That's a pretty name."

I'd walked off from Buck and Johntay and had rolled right up on Cash, who was still loading her plate up with food in the line.

"Thanks," she said dryly.

"For a person with such an ugly attitude."

"What?" she asked, damn near spitting out her soda.

"You hear me, shawty."

She knew damn well she heard me, but I figured I'd repeat myself so she didn't think that I had a problem doing so.

"That name is too pretty for its owner to have such an ugly attitude. What's that about, huh?" I asked.

While she sat there with her mouth open, I figured I'd use the time to greet her friend, since she was standing right beside Cash, staring me in my damn mouth.

"How you doing?" I asked.

"I'm fine," she said, a little too friendly for me.

Her response almost came out flirtatiously. I kept an even face as I made a mental note to watch her pasty-looking ass. Especially because it was evident that my interest was clearly in her friend, and she was standing there looking like she was ready to pull a nigga's pants down and eat the dick up. I'd seen and been with a lot of bitches in my last two years as a free man, and bitches like her were conniving.

"That's good," I finally said to homegirl.

I turned my attention back to Cash, who was now out the line and headed to a table.

"So, you not gon' answer my question?" I asked, following her.

"In my opinion, I don't have an ugly attitude, but I can't change your perception."

"Well, actually, you could."

Cash rolled her eyes and took a seat at an empty table that Fa Ma had set up so people could sit down, eat, drink, and play cards.

"I don't care to."

I smirked as she looked at me with an attitude. I didn't usually pursue broads, but it was something about Cash that made me want to tame her smart-ass mouth. It was like she was always on defense. Normally a bitch with that kind of attitude would get cursed out so bad that she'd be in tears, but I liked Cash. I truly believed that under her tough exterior, there was something soft.

"Can I take you out on a date?" I asked, getting straight to the point. I was done with all the back and forth.

"I'm good," she quickly said.

"No, you not. But you could be better if you fucked with me."

"I'm good," she repeated.

"You like yo' job?"

"Yeah, it's alright. I need it more than anything," she said.

I looked in her eyes after she said it and I couldn't help but pick up on a little sadness. Something was going on with her. I looked at Cash's plate. It was piled high. I was about to say something slick, but I had a gut feeling I shouldn't.

"Say yes to the date or I'll make you lose that job. I'll have Fat Ma fire you for the way you treated me the other day in the store."

I was lying, but she wouldn't be able to say no if I backed her into a corner. Cash had been forking at her food and taking bites but stopped abruptly after I gave her that ultimatum.

"Are you fucking serious?" she asked in disbelief. Her homegirl also stared at me like I was tripping. Her mouth was damn near hanging open. She didn't say anything though, because I flashed her a look daring her to.

"Yeah. No is never an option for me. Take the date or lose your job. It's your choice." I shrugged.

She glared at me before sighing angrily.

"Super corny, but you got that. I'll take the date." I could tell that the irritation she was showing was genuine, but I didn't really give a fuck.

"Call my phone and shoot me your address. I'll pick you up later."

"Later?" she asked. "I need time to get myself together."

"Okay, well your time starts now. Eat ya plate, pack some leftovers, and ditch this broad. You got two hours."

Cash stared at me like she wanted to pop off, but she agreed because she had no other choice. I rambled off my number, she called me, and then I headed back to Fat Ma's house. It wasn't shit else at that kickback I needed.

Chapter 10
Cashmere

Not even an hour and a half had passed since Wolf had damn near blackmailed me for my phone number. Although he'd originally asked for my address, I didn't give it to him. I agreed to meet him in front of Fat Ma's store. I couldn't lie, he was handsome, but he was arrogant, persistent, and downright annoying. I didn't like being forced into anything and he was pushing every button I had. After taking a few plates to go, I had Izzy drop me off at my house. She was one of the few people that knew where I lived at. My grandmama's house was in the cut on a side road luckily, so it wasn't too many people that came up and down the street. The folks living on the road were old and most of them were living off some type of government check.

My phone dinged as I walked back toward Fat Ma's store.

I'm waiting.

That was the text that Wolf had sent me. Ten minutes ago, he'd sent me one, asking if I was ready. The nigga was impatient too. A part of me just wanted to tell Fat Ma what had happened. She always valued honesty. Plus, I didn't like anyone trying to hang anything over my head like he was doing.

Every part of me was nervous and with each step, I contemplated turning around. *What the fuck did Wolf see in me? Why did he want to talk to me? Was it because I was a virgin and someone had told him?*

A lot of the dudes in Oakdale stepped to me solely for that reason. I hated that Beetlesburg was such a small town, and everybody knew everybody's business. Yeah, virginity was rare nowadays. A poppin' pussy was glorified and noted as being a for sure way out of poverty, but I wasn't falling for that. I wanted to do something else with my life. I wasn't sure what that was, but I knew fucking and sucking niggas' dicks wasn't going to be it.

There were whispers going around that my sister and her friends were chasing the Atlanta dream, and everyone knew what that consisted off. Shaking ass and finding a baller. Missing my sister and wondering what the hell happened to her made me want to keep my legs closed even tighter. I was going to rise up using my brain. As I walked, I reminded myself not to get caught up in Wolf's lies. Although they hadn't come yet, I knew they would. That's exactly how shit started with Jermaine. He was all nice in the beginning and then his true colors surfaced. I'd learned that you had to give people time. If someone was being fake, let them, because they would only be able to hold it up for so long.

A few minutes later, I came up on Fat Ma's store. I hadn't bothered to text Wolf back. As I approached I spotted him on the hood of a big, black, fancy-looking car.

"'Bout time!" he called out.

"You said two hours. It's only been one and a half, and let's not forget you were texting me in one."

He smiled and allowed his eyes to roam my body shamelessly.

"I love that mouth, girl," he said.

I couldn't help but shake my head while he opened the passenger door for me to get in.

"You look nice," he said after closing my door and hopping in.

"Thank you."

I was glad that he noticed the effort. I didn't have many nice clothes, but I did have a cute little dress that Izzy had given to me that she could no longer fit. My grandmama had shown me how to sew years back before she became bed ridden and I continued to brush up on my skills. I took the dress, cut off some of the fabric, and brought in the waistline so it hugged my body nicely.

"Your car is nice," I told him.

"Thank you," he replied as he strapped on his seatbelt.

"What kind is it? It smells funny."

I asked because the inside was ridiculously large and the interior was two different colors and materials. Cream and a shiny, wood-like texture made up the inside.

"It's a Bentley. I try not to do too much when I come back home. And what you smell is genuine leather."

I nodded, not really caring one way or another. I just wanted to get this little date over and done with so I could get back home.

Wolf and I ended up at a small, twenty-four-hour-diner a few towns over. I texted Izzy my location and then told myself I was going to make a conscious effort to have fun and enjoy the date. I didn't get out much and after about a half hour with Wolf, I realized he wasn't so bad. He wasn't invasive, didn't ask a ton of questions, and focused more on just cracking jokes so I would smile. He kept telling me that it was okay to be myself and laugh a little, so I did just that. He let me order what I wanted and when he sensed that I was being modest, he overordered so I could try several different things. He talked about himself a little. Told me he did a stint in juvie and was actually smart and probably could have gone to college on a full scholarship if he had applied himself. He spoke about chemistry, which I thought was odd for a black guy, and he spoke about his mom dying from cancer. Said it changed him.

Wolf's openness put me at ease, and I eventually spoke on my parents being killed when I was younger, and my grand-mama raising us the best she could. I even told him about Satin. At the end of the night, I had an entirely new perception of Wolf. He still exhibited jerk-like tendencies, but knowing he too had experienced some loss and sadness in the past made me a little more tolerant of him. A part of him was very kind, and the way he spoke about his mother and Fat Ma, I could tell he loved them and respected women very much. It was refreshing to be able to peel back his layers. I was curious to see what else was there.

Two slices of pie, two milkshakes, and four entrees later, it was time to go.

"Thank you," I said out the blue as Wolf drove us back to Beetlesburg.

He had the radio down very low and appeared to be in thought. With the car so quiet, I figured I'd use the time to thank him. He'd shown me a good time and he allowed me to take home all the leftovers. Along with the plates from the barbecue, my grandmama and I would be eating good for the next couple of days.

We got back on the main road of Beetlesburg about ten minutes later, and while I expected Wolf to drop me off in front of Fat Ma's, he insisted on taking me back to my house.

"I already told you I wasn't comfortable with that," I said sternly.

I didn't understand why he would fuck up a good night with that request after I'd already told him no. As usual, he was being hella pushy and persistent, but I was so embarrassed about my living situation that this time, I wasn't budging.

Chapter 11
Ezekiel "Wolf" Griffin

"I'm taking you home, Cash. What's the issue with your crib?" I asked, getting right to the point.

I had picked her up from the store like she insisted, and now she wasn't trying to let me drop her off at her crib. It was damn near midnight and there was no way in hell that I was dropping her back off in front of the store for her to walk home.

Cash was acting hella weird about letting a nigga come through her crib. I had a feeling that shawty lived in deep poverty and she was scared to be vulnerable with me. I respected it but I didn't like that shit. I liked Cash, but I didn't like that she felt like she couldn't be her whole self with me or reveal her struggles with me. I knew it was early, but I wanted her to trust me. I wasn't about to judge her, and my own past experiences would never allow me to look down on her. I might have gone about a couple things wrong when it came to her, but I meant well and my intentions were good. Of course, at times it was hard communicating that shit. I was dominant by nature, didn't like motherfuckers telling me no, and I preferred to call the shots.

"There's no issue, just drop me off at the store."

"No," I said flatly.

"I'll be fine, Wolf."

"I said no. You act like I wanna come in the house or some shit. I ain't ask to meet nobody. I just want you to get home safe."

"No, Wolf. Just drop me off at the store. Damn." She let out an exasperated sigh like I was annoying her.

"Nah, fuck that. I'm not trying to hear it. What's the problem? Ya house fucked up? That's what it is?"

She didn't respond. She just sat there looking stupid as shit. She was really starting to irritate me, and I was having a hard time concealing the shit. The nice-guy shit was definitely about to go out the window.

"I don't give a fuck if yo' house is a shack, shawty. You act like I'm gon' judge you. I keep telling you, I'm not like these lame-ass niggas around here. How the fuck we gon' build a bond if you don't let a nigga in?" I questioned with passion roaring in my eyes.

Cash blinked back tears as she responded.

"Build a bond? You barely fuckin' know me!" she argued, getting upset for no damn reason. "And how you know I want to build a bond with you?"

"I don't give a fuck what you want. It's what you need. You lonely mama, and you guarded. But you don't need to be that way with me. Now, tell me the address or I'm gon' call Fat Ma and get it from her. You know she gon' give it to me."

Just like I was never going to get Cash fired, I was never going to call Fat Ma either. I just knew that throwing her name up in there would make Cash do what I wanted a little quicker.

I was persistent either way, so I was going to get what I wanted, no matter what.

"Now all of a sudden you know what I need." She shook her head and scoffed lightly. "But, okay," she said, before rambling off the address.

A few minutes later, I pulled up to her crib. It was at the very end of a raggedy little street that I'd never even noticed. Of course, it was dark when we arrived, but with my lights illuminating against the house, I could see it as clear as day. To be truthful, the spot resembled a shack. Just like I expected. It was nearly dilapidated and almost leaning to the side. The lawn was unkept with the grass appearing to be damn near to a mafucka ankles.

"Now was that so hard?" I asked, using my finger to nudge her cheek.

She snatched her face back and rolled her eyes. I didn't care though. Grabbing all the bags containing the leftovers, she noisily got out of the car and headed into the house. I couldn't help but smile. Although I knew she was annoyed with me, I still felt good chilling with her for the little bit of time that I did. Cash was cool as shit, and we were similar in more ways than one. She needed someone just like I did and after a while, the walls would come down and the attitude would leave with them. I smiled at the thought. I had no doubt that Cash was going to be around for a while.

* * *

"What's going on with you and Cash?" Fat Ma asked the next morning.

I was sleeping in the old bedroom that I used to have when I stayed with her after my mama died. The same room that I used to share with Kwame when he came over. I'd barely gotten the chance to open my eyes. I guessed she'd heard me ruffling around on that squeaky ass mattress that she needed to replace.

"Damn, Fat Ma. Can I wake up?"

"Yo' eyes is open, ain't they?" she countered, matching my sarcasm. "If yo' eyes open, then you open. Besides, it's damn near the afternoon. You wanted to be out half the night and think you gon' sleep in half the morning. Don't work like that."

I let out a deep yawn, pushed my arms out in a Y to stretch, and then smiled. My grandma got on my nerves, but I loved her to death.

"I took her out to eat. Is that okay with you?" I asked, finally sitting all the way up and bringing my feet off the bed and to the floor.

"No, it's not all right. You know full well who that child is," she said sternly.

I didn't respond. I just looked at her.

"Don't give me that look, Ezekiel."

I was getting on her nerves. She only called me by my government name when she was mad at me.

"You and I both know that before you do anything, you do your research. You're very intelligent and have been since I known ya."

"Okay, so I know who she is. What that mean?"

My eyes met her gaze and I waited for her to respond. Of course, she was right, I figured out who she was when I put two and two together. It drew me to her even more because we had so much in common. More than we knew. A nigga didn't necessarily believe in fate, but I did believe that sometimes people were meant to cross paths.

"It means ... be careful with her. She didn't get a Fat Ma when she lost her mama and daddy. She got a life of hardship right after and it didn't get any better since then. If you gon' bother that gal, make sure you have good intentions. You understand?" she asked sternly.

"Yes ma'am."

I smiled at her but she didn't smile back.

"I mean it, Wolf. If you don't want her, leave her be. If you do want her, then treat her right. Trust me, after the life she's had, she deserves it."

"Well, who better to give it to her than me?"

"Mmmm hhhm. That sho' would be a blessing, 'cause lawd knows I love that child. I ain't gon' get in the way of y'all getting to know each other. I just ask that you be good to her."

"Yes ma'am," I told her again before she finally headed toward the door.

"Since you professing yo' love today, you gon' show ya grandson you love him by making him breakfast fit for a king?"

Finally, her fat, chocolate cheeks turned up into the smile I'd been waiting on.

"Sure suga'. By the time you wash up, Fat Ma will have some breakfast made for you."

Hearing Fat Ma say that did have me looking at Cash in an even more positive light. Don't get it twisted, a nigga's heart was ice cold because most motherfuckers weren't worthy of warmth. Fat Ma was good to everybody, but she wouldn't go as far to say she loved folks that weren't blood. That spoke volumes. I did plan to kick it with Cash more. I liked shawty and the way she grew up had her appreciative of the smallest things. Being around arrogant-ass niggas all day made me appreciate her humility. People like her were the ones you blessed in abundance because they appreciated it the most.

Chapter 12
Cashmere "Cash" Ellis

"You never been to Atlanta?" Wolf asked.

A few days had passed since our first date at the diner, and I had a day off, so Wolf hit me up and suggested we have a second date together. I was all for it, because to be honest, I couldn't get enough of seeing his fine, chocolate self. He had his moments of meanness, but he was funny, and he kept me company at the store. I actually looked forward to seeing him.

Since the diner, he'd been coming by the store a lot to just sit, talk, and occasionally steal. His ass knew he would come in there and start eating things like he'd paid for it. Fat Ma didn't seem to mind, so I no longer bothered trying to stop him.

According to Fat Ma, he was only supposed to be in town a short while, but he had extended his stay. I wasn't sure why, and although Fat Ma's cute little grin implied that it was because of me, I still couldn't understand. I was cute, but I was so damn basic compared to him. With his smooth, black skin, charm, and devilish grin, he could have had the baddest chick in Atlanta. For the life of me, I couldn't understand why he wanted to hang out with me.

"Actually ... I've never been out of Beetlesburg," I finally admitted.

I had gotten lost for a minute, gazing at him.

"Well, ride out with me for a day. Something came up and I need a riding patna."

"That's cool with me. Let me just get my grandmama situated and I'll meet you at the store."

"Here we go with that shit again," he said. "I'm picking you up from yo' crib. Be ready in an hour."

Wolf didn't bother to wait for an answer. He simply hung up. I exhaled and sat my phone down on the mattress I slept on. I didn't have a whole bed. Just a mattress. But I wasn't about to complain.

I checked on my grandmama, making sure she had enough to drink by her bedside. She had her oxygen machine, a few snacks, and something to watch on television. She was good with taking her own medicine as long as it was close by. There wasn't more that I could do for her, other than help make her comfortable. She didn't want anyone helping her wash up, so she bathed herself to the best of her ability whenever she felt like it. She often smelled, but I didn't say anything; I couldn't disrespect the woman that had raised me.

"I'm gonna head out for a little bit. I'll be back in later."

I was standing over her bed talking to her, but I didn't expect her to respond. It took a lot out of her just to breathe these days, so she didn't do too much talking.

"You have everything you need. I'll lock the door and I'll see you later."

She mumbled a faint 'okay,' and then I pressed my lips into her forehead and took off toward the front door to wait for Wolf.

When Satin first left, my grandmama didn't really want me going too many places after that. It was hard, especially because Nook literally went right behind her. Her body was failing her, and she was frustrated that all she could literally and physically do was sit, worry, and wonder. With the little bit of energy she had, she would try to argue to keep me in the house, but I couldn't stay. Most of her income was tied up in her medicine. The healthcare system was horrible in Georgia, and it was either purchase what she needed or she would die. I needed to work, and there was no way I was going to pass up on the job offer Fat Ma had given me.

Before I could get too deep in thought, the sound of Wolf's car coming down the gravel road sent me rushing out the door. However, the bag on the front porch sent me quickly rushing back in. Otis had made his monthly drop off and Wolf seeing a bag of food sitting outside for us had my face flushed hot. It was embarrassing and I made a mental note to tell his ass to cut it out.

After taking the bag back inside, I hopped in Wolf's car and we were off.

"What types of things do you like to do?" he asked me a few minutes into the drive.

He hadn't said anything about the bag, so I figured, maybe he hadn't noticed it. I tried to focus on his question but sadly, it was hard to answer. I grew quiet and thought for a few minutes. I wasn't sure. I'd never really had the opportunity to do anything significant.

"I haven't really done much," I admitted.

"Well, what do you like? What would you like to try?"

"Beetlesburg doesn't have much. Most of the time when I'm not working, I'm reading. I love books. I go to the library and dig through the little that they have."

Wolf briefly took his eyes off the road and stole a glance at me.

"Oh, you a bookworm. What kind of books?"

"Black romance. I used to read a lot of urban, but I got tired of reading about drug dealers who swoop in and save the day. That shit ain't realistic, so I began reading more love stories."

"Drug dealers saving the day and changing a bitch life ain't realistic but a fuckin' love story is?" Wolf laughed.

"In my opinion, yes. The love stories are a lot more realistic. They're usually just two regular people who fall in love. I enjoy that better."

"Is that right?" he asked. "With that being said, I think I know a few places we can go."

* * *

Wolf took me to the Barnes and Noble near the Cumberland Mall in Atlanta. I knew it because I saw the big sign close by. I was in awe when I walked in. The place was huge, had two floors, and more books than I'd ever seen in one place. The library in Beetlesburg was tiny and I never imagined that a bookstore that big even existed. The best part of the visit was when he told me to 'get what you want.' I wasn't greedy by a long shot, but hearing those words was music to my ears. Outside of the library, books were a luxury in my household. I ended up walking out with a bag full of books, a couple cookies, and an overpriced latte. By the time we left, I was high off the experience and Wolf was looking at me like I'd officially lost it.

"I see you enjoying yourself," Wolf said, eyeing my bag.

"I am. I really appreciate this, Wolf. Thank you."

He smiled. "You appreciate it, huh? Well, I'm just getting started."

I could only imagine what else he had up his sleeve, but I

found out not long after exactly what Wolf had up his sleeve when we pulled up to a fancy-looking restaurant. The place was called Nikolai's and it was located on the thirtieth floor of the building. It was beautiful inside with warm lights and twinkling candles throughout. Large windows that gave a breathtaking view of Atlanta's skyline.

My eyes widened and I couldn't help but be captivated by the view. I had never seen anything like it or been anywhere as nice as it. I was beginning to wonder if maybe those urban books were actually more realistic than what I thought. Wolf flashed me a charming grin as he watched me take it all in, and I felt a flutter in my chest. When the hostess approached us, he motioned us toward the table with a sweep of his hand.

"You like it?" Wolf asked after we settled in our seats by the window.

My voice caught in my throat before I could answer and after a few seconds of silence, it returned.

"It's... it's incredible."

He chuckled, his eyes never leaving mine.

"Fat Ma told me that if I came at you, then I'd better come correct."

We both laughed because I knew damn well she didn't say that.

"She didn't say it in those words, but she definitely said some similar shit."

I was touched that Fat Ma had made it a priority to talk to Wolf about me. I felt important and I was thankful, because she knew better than anyone that I didn't have the space in my heart for more disappointment and pain.

"I gotta be honest, Wolf," I started, fidgeting with my napkin. "I never thought I'd end up on a rooftop like this with someone like you. This is like a dream," I admitted.

He raised an eyebrow, his gaze intense. "And what do you mean by 'someone like me,' Cash?"

I blushed, realizing I might have come off a bit judgmental. "I mean, you're you, and I'm... well, I'm just me."

"Who am I?" he asked.

I shrugged because truthfully, I had no idea, but I still tried to articulate what I thought.

"I don't know ... You look like you got yourself together. You dress nice. You can come and go as you please and money doesn't seem to be a worry. And you're handsome," I admitted for the first time. "I just don't get why you've taken an interest in me."

"I'm just Wolf. And you and I, Cash, are equals. My story is fucked up too and I've gone through some things as well. And don't ever say you're 'just you' again."

There it was. That dominant personality that I couldn't help but find attractive.

He leaned forward and looked me dead in my eyes.

"You're more than 'just you,' Cash. You're smart, strong, and you've got this humble way of seeing the world, and I admire that."

I swallowed hard, my heart skipping a beat. "You really think so?"

Wolf nodded, sincerity shining in his eyes.

A waiter in a tuxedo holding a silver tray with fancy glasses of ice water appeared before us to greet us and take our orders. I let Wolf order for me since I had no idea what half that shit on the menu was. I ended up with lamb chops, asparagus, and creamy mashed potatoes. The lamb chops and asparagus were new to me, and I was hesitant. However, Wolf and the fancy-looking waiter assured me that I would like it.

Once he was gone, I decided to learn more about Wolf. We'd grown a lot over the last couple of days but to be honest, I didn't know much about him. I didn't know anything about his parents or what he did for a living. *Did he have children or a girl back in Atlanta?* I was starting to like him, and I needed those questions answered.

"Wolf, whatever happened to your parents? I know you said Fat Ma raised you."

"My mom was brutally raped while she was fighting cancer."

"Oh my god!" I said, my hand flying to my mouth in disbelief.

I looked around to make sure that I hadn't been too loud. I didn't want all those white folks in our business. And that was exactly what color nearly everyone in there was.

Wolf shrugged and gave me a blank look. I knew that look. It was one that people wore when they were trying to hide pain. I wore it daily.

"I ain't gon' lie, it fucked me up. But over time it got easier."

"You had a sister too?" I asked.

I remembered him mentioning having a sister before. I figured if I was going to ask him to relive some bad memories, it would be better if he did it all at once.

Wolf nodded. "My sister was raped the same night with my mother. She killed herself a few days after being released from the hospital. Couldn't handle the flashbacks."

Out of instinct, I reached over the table and grabbed the hand he had resting there. Again, I told him I was sorry, and he flashed a weak smile.

"The crazy part was they didn't do shit to anybody. My pops was out here robbing people so he could get money to buy the cancer meds that my mother's insurance wouldn't pay for, and she ended up losing her life behind it. The life that he was ironically trying to preserve."

I pulled my hand back, shook my head, and released a heavy sigh.

"Shit fucked us both up. Me and him. We just decided to cope differently."

"Where's your dad now?"

"He around. But I don't fuck with that nigga."

My eyes studied Wolf and I could sense his mood had darkened. Just that quick. I decided I wouldn't pry any more that night. Him sharing what he did was more than enough for me.

Our food came out shortly after and Wolf was right. I enjoyed every drop of it, leaving none to even take home. When it was time to pay, the waiter brought the bill out and handed it directly to Wolf, but I managed to steal a glance at it. It was nearly several hundred dollars. He paid cash and left a tip. What he did for a living now really sat at the forefront of my mind. Most people were struggling to bring that home in a week or two. There he was spending that type of money on a meal. I had told myself that I wasn't going to ask, but I had to. The rumors were that my mama and daddy had been killed because someone was trying to get to his drug money. I didn't want any parts of that lifestyle. I just hoped that Wolf wasn't into that, because I was really starting to like him.

Chapter 13
Senator "Sin" Jones

"Remember me?" I asked the nigga in the yard after jumping out the passenger seat of the black Charger my little homie O was driving.

After dropping a bag on his head, I'd gotten his location from his own cousin. It never ceased to amaze me how niggas would slime their own family out if the money was right. He'd been hiding out at his auntie's house after shuffling all over the city. Running to defend his thieving, hoe-ass cousin was going to cost him his life. I'd barely let the car roll to a complete stop. Just the sight of his ass had my adrenaline roaring at 100 percent. I was so charged up, it literally had my dick hard. I'd been looking for his bitch ass for several weeks and after seeing him, the rush I'd been longing for hit me hard. The nigga had shot at me and my patna and now he was about to pay with his life in the worst way. Either he thought shit was sweet or he really didn't know who the fuck Wolf Pack niggas were.

Remember me? As soon as the question left my mouth, the nigga took off running. He was so quick that if I had blinked, I would have missed the fear flicker in his eyes. That would have been disappointing since I wanted to enjoy every second of torturing his ass mentally and physically.

"Don't run, Dante!" I called him by his government, taunting him.

I knew more about him than his mama probably knew. I knew he was twenty-five, had two baby mamas and another little bitch pregnant out in Douglasville. He sold powder, tricked heavy, and ran with a gang called DB. Short for Diego brothers. He'd shot at me for throwing his thieving ass cousin out of my house naked, but when I caught up with his ass, he was going to wish that he'd stayed out my fuckin' business.

"Catch his ass!" I ordered to the three young niggas O and I had brought with us.

They were the newest to The Wolf Pack and they were also the youngest. I was hoping that they would also be the fastest. I wanted this nigga Dante like yesterday, and I was going to be super pissed if I didn't leave with his ass. I had plans of watching him die in the worst way.

As soon as I barked the command, both passenger doors of the Charger flew open and the two youngins hopped out the cars and sprinted in the same direction as Dante. I pulled my gun out and then sprinted behind them. I knew he was alone so I wasn't worried about him having anyone close by that would wage war behind him. I pulled out my gun because the pussy was kind of fast, and I'd gun him down before I lost him.

With my Glock in my hand, I did a light run in the direction that Dante and my little homies had gone. I didn't have to go far. They'd already caught him. While Dante lay on the ground and let out groans, the two young niggas beat his ass. I'm talking fist and feet.

"Good job, but don't waste your energy beating on him. Drag his ass back to the car and throw that nigga in the trunk."

They immediately did as told, but Dante decided he wasn't

going out without a fight. I didn't have time for the silly shit, so I aimed down and promptly shot his ass in the leg.

"The next shot will be yo' arm, nigga," I told him as he roared in pain.

That didn't stop my guys from dragging him across that ground and then getting his arms and feet and tossing his bloody ass in the trunk.

"What you plan to do with him, Sin?" one of the young boys eagerly asked from the backseat.

He went by Pit. Not sure why he chose it, but the name fit the little nigga. A short, stocky nigga that wore two braids down each side of his head, he did kinda remind me of a dog.

"Nigga, don't ever ask a big homie no shit like that! If he want you to know, he'll tell you."

O's message came out aggressive as fuck but for good reasons. It just wasn't some shit you asked.

"My bad, fam," he said apologetically.

"I told you about that shit, nigga. You asking like you the mafuckin' police, nigga."

"Shut the fuck up, nigga," Pit barked back irritably. "I said my bad."

"Facts," O continued. "I done had to holla at you about that shit before too, so we don't need you chiming in. Just do as y'all told and sit the fuck back."

Neither of them said a word. They just complied and remained silent the rest of the way.

"Aye, I got that," I said to Wolf after he answered his phone on the second ring.

He already knew what I was talking about, so I didn't go into detail and he didn't ask no questions. He knew that Dante's cousin was in the process of telling me where that nigga was. It was actually the same bitch I threw out that day. She claimed she never intended for no shit like that to happen and she only called him to step to me. I knew the bitch was lying to save her own ass because just like Dante, I planned to lay her ass down the first chance I got. A couple niggas had died behind that shit. We were gunning at any and everybody Wolf and I ever had beef with. We didn't give a fuck. And Wolf was big on if you crossed us, then you had to pay. That bitch was no exception.

"Where to take him?" I asked Wolf.

"Breeding ground."

A smile crept up on my face. The breeding ground was a special place for Wolf. It was also a special place for a nigga like me because I loved to see what happened to motherfuckers that violated. Wolf wanted to set an example with this nigga, and I was all for it.

"Head back to the spot so I can drop you little niggas off," I said to O.

Outside of Wolf and Cheese, I was the only one who knew about the breeding ground.

"Cool," O responded to my demand with a nod.

Although they weren't sure how it would happen, they all knew that it would be the last time anyone would ever see Dante's bitch ass alive again.

Chapter 14
Ezekiel "Wolf" Griffin

"Why do you have a gun out?" Cash asked in a whisper through the window she had cracked.

We had left the restaurant and were about to head back to Beetlesburg, but my gaslight had popped on so I stopped to the convenience store.

"You been asking a whole lot of questions tonight," I said with a smirk. While she stared at me from a half-open passenger window, I did a slow turn to every angle of my body in order to do a quick scan of my surroundings.

"Atlanta is a different type of city. You look down and somebody be done ran up on you and took your shit," I finally replied.

"Your car?"

Her eyes bucked and then she rolled her window back up. I noticed that she'd begun to look around cautiously as well. She was a fast learner. I liked that.

I finished pumping my gas, returned the nozzle to its base, and then hopped back in the car.

"You on point now I see," I said through a chuckle.

She nodded but didn't visibly relax until I'd pulled out of the parking lot and got back on the road.

"There's nothing to be nervous about. I don't want you out here all scared. Just be cautious. When you start driving, I'll make sure you're licensed and trained to carry, and I'll make sure other motherfuckers that put in that type of work know you are."

"When I start driving? Boy please. Driving school is an arm and a leg and I don't even have a license. Shit, I don't even know how to drive. My grandmama ain't never own no car."

"Stop worrying about the small things. You stick around me long enough and you'll have what you need."

She got quiet and remained that way until we were off the main streets and back on the expressway.

"Wolf, what do you do for work?" she blurted out.

I stared ahead. I knew that was coming.

"I work in pharmaceuticals."

"You mean drugs?" she asked, staring at me blankly.

"Yeah. Real drugs though. You know I'm part African," I told her.

When the words came out, I was dead serious but for some reason, she began to laugh.

"What's funny?" I asked. "I was serious. My mom came to the US twenty-some years ago on a school visa. She was a biochemistry major at Spelman. Her dream was to be a biochemist then go back home and help create medicine to save kids in those fucked-up remote villages back in her home. What I'm getting at is that smart shit comes naturally to a nigga."

"So your mom was a super-smart African chick. So, how did she get with your dad? I'm assuming he was from here."

I nodded.

"Yeah. He was smart too. He was going to nearby Georgia Tech. Only he was on a sports scholarship. Basketball. They met, started kicking it, and here I come. Her family was mad as hell. Tried to get her to get rid of me because they knew it would fuck up her education. She wouldn't and they disowned her. It was her and my dad after that. She literally had no family in the states. They came back to stay with my grandma and both started working at Donaldson's."

"The beef plant?" she asked.

I nodded.

"My mom was supposed to be the first to go back to school and finish her degree and then my dad was supposed to go back. Never happened. Before I even started crawling, she was pregnant with my sister. Now it's two kids and bills won't stop coming. And then my mom was diagnosed with cancer. She beat it and then it came back. School became a distant memory for the two of them and their focus became survival."

"Damn," she said solemnly. "It sounds like you came from a good home, so why don't you like your dad?"

I let out a sigh and grew quiet, staring ahead as I continued down the expressway. Finally responding, I told her, "I don't want to talk about that nigga right now. I'm just telling you my history, but I don't want to get into all of why I don't fuck with him."

"Okay," she said with a little bit of an attitude. I noticed she had fallen back further into the passenger seat and instead of her body leaning toward me, it was now leaning toward the window.

"Going back to what I do. You ever heard of Viagra?"

"Viagra?"

"Yeah."

"I've heard about it. A few books I read mentioned the guys using it. What about it?"

"Well, Viagra was originally released under a different name for treatment of high blood pressure and heart disease.

So, when doctors found out it caused niggas' dicks to get hard, they started selling it for that as well. Named it Viagra."

"Okay."

She had no clue what I was getting at.

"I created a drug, Cash. So, quick story. Just like the adult prisons, the boot camp I was held at was full of a bunch of niggas from the streets. They had shit in common, like they fought, hung out, and a lot of them sold drugs while they were on the street. A lot of them also got high. You know ... Some of them smoked a little weed. Some of them sniffed a little cocaine. So, me being me, I was always the one in there taking shit, putting it together, and playing around. They had me cleaning when I was locked up. Everyone had a job. Mine was to clean. That exposed me to chemicals that I would steal. With my chemistry background I began to concoct shit. I ended up creating something that niggas could get high off of. It started off in powder form and I sold it to the other inmates. The niggas were going crazy over the shit. I knew I was gonna be a rich motherfucker when I got out. There were some effects that I couldn't fucking understand. It not only got folks high, but it was also lowering niggas' cholesterol. Significantly. When I got out, I sold some regular drugs to get my money up, and eventually I got in a real lab that I rented, took the components I learned in jail, and recreated the drug I'd made. I removed a couple of things and pitched it to a few pharmaceutical companies as a cholesterol-lowering drug."

"And they took it?"

"Yep. They took it. From me, an untrained chemist with not a single fucking credential. They knew they could make money off it and that's all those companies worry about. They brought me in and I got up in their labs to work with their people, showing them how to recreate it. That was successful. They offered me a lump sun but I also asked for 10 percent of the first year's sales and then 1 percent every year for the next twenty years. It was scraps compared to what they would make over time. At the end of the day, I walked away with 1.5 billion dollars."

Cash just stared at me. I knew what I was telling her wasn't registering in that pretty little head of hers.

"You're a billionaire?" she finally asked as it registered.

"Yeah, give or take. They raped a nigga in taxes. You the first person I ever broke this shit down to, and I only did that because I fuck with you, and I believe I can trust you a little. My cousin Kwame knows because he negotiated everything as my lawyer. Not even Senator knew how wealthy I was. The entire deal was classified, with iron-clad contracts and non-disclosure agreements signed."

She mouthed the word 'wow' and let everything that I had said sink in. It was still sinking in for me actually. The deal had just happened a little less than a year ago. It was in the works around the time Cheese disappeared. It was crazy that I was filthy fucking rich but none of it meant shit. If I could give every dollar up to get my mom and sister back, I would. Shit, I would even give it up to have my daddy back. Back when I was proud to call him my pops.

None of the money meant a damn thing when you had nothing to live for. No family. I had Fat Ma and I loved her, but I kept my distance from the town she lived in out of mental necessity. Sin was like the closest thing to family that I had other than Tara and the kids.

"Can I ask you something?" I asked, changing the tone of the conversation.

Although I'd shared my financial status with her, she wasn't truly grasping how much of an impact it would have on her own life. She would later, but for now I decided to ask her some questions.

"Depends. What is it?"

"Why you ain't never fuck before?"

"What kind of question is that?"

"I'm just asking, damn. You ask me hella personal shit and I don't say shit."

"Yeah, and you don't answer everything either." She rolled her eyes.

I laughed to put her at ease. I didn't want any smoke.

"Just like I had a choice, so do you. You ain't gotta answer the shit."

She let out an annoyed breath and then answered.

"I had other shit to worry about. When you worrying about how to stop ya fucking stomach from growling, the last thing you gonna be thinking about is allowing someone to fuck you for their pleasure."

"Their pleasure?" Wolf countered.

"Yeah, they're pleasure."

"Hmm."

"Hmm what?"

"Someone told you that fucking wasn't pleasurable?"

"I told myself, Wolf. What would I get out of letting someone stick their dick in and out of me? I have so much negative shit going on, there's no way I can find pleasure in that."

"So, you're saying, you won't have sex until your life is together?"

"I didn't say that. I said I had so much negative shit going on. Life is bigger than Beetlesburg and sex is a distraction. I gotta focus on all these negatives and make something positive happen. I just can't lay up and screw when my life is shit."

I nodded because I definitely understood.

"Nah, you're right. But I got another question for you," I told her, my face growing serious.

"Okay."

"What if a nigga changed that? Sex would no longer be a distraction and then you would indulge in it?" I asked.

"Is that all you want? You heard I was a virgin and wanted to fuck. Just like all the other niggas around there."

I laughed, slightly offended. I wasn't shit like those other niggas.

"I can get sex from anybody. It's rare that I feel a connection. Do I like you? Absolutely. Do I want to fuck you ... Hell yeah. And yes, I heard you were a virgin, but that ain't why I stepped to you."

She rolled her eyes and mumbled a whatever.

"I just want a better life and that's all I'm focused on."

I couldn't help but grow annoyed. Cash wasn't getting it. I just told her dumb ass that I had cash out the ass and she was talking about being focused on a better life. I was the better life. She'd came up but she had no fucking idea. Just when I was about to tell her how simple she was acting, my phone began to ring. I answered it. It was Sin and he had some good news.

"Take him to the breeding ground," I told him before hanging up. "Some important shit just came up. There's been a change of plans," I told her as I immediately began to reroute. I looked at the signs on the road and began heading to the closest hotel. "I'm gonna drop you off at a hotel and I'll be back."

Fear flashed in her eyes. "Drop me off at a hotel? Oh hell no! Take me home, Wolf. I don't want to be in a strange place by myself. If you drop me off, how do I know if you're gonna come back and get me? I'll be stranded. I don't have much money," she said as if I were completely unaware of that. "Oh my god! If I offended you, I'm sorry!"

"What are you talking about, shawty?" I asked, growing annoyed. I just got the best news I'd heard in weeks and she was acting all retarded because a nigga was about to drop her off for a few hours in a hotel. "Ain't nobody finna have you stranded. Matter fact."

With my hand still on the steering wheel, I leaned slightly on her side, reached down, and opened the glove compartment above her legs. When it popped open there were two big, thick wads of money.

"You a cashier so I know you can count. Take either of those rolls and peel off a thousand dollars for yourself. You keep that. It's yours. That way you have enough money to catch a cab back to Beetlesburg. You won't need it, but at least you'll have peace of mind knowing you can't be stranded because you have cash. I'll pay for the room and like I said, I'll be back."

Her anxiety died down instantly as she grabbed the roll closest to her and peeled off the money.

"Now, let me get you settled, so I can handle this business."

* * *

"Please man! It wasn't me!"

I stood in front of the man who had shot at me and grinned as he begged for his life. I didn't speak. I never did when someone was about to die. Instead, I chose to remain silent. I wanted to hear, see, and smell the fear in my prey. I did that best when I said nothing and just observed.

"Nigga, we looked right at yo' dumb ass," Senator told him. He was right. He and his patna had on masks, but we already had confirmation that he was the primary culprit. We didn't have the other nigga's name, but we would by the time we were done with his ass.

"See what you thought was, you had one up on us and you were ready to put a nigga's lights out. But you slipped."

"Please fam. I'll do whatever. What I need to do?"

Sin looked at me and a smile stretched across his face.

"Two things. One, tell us the name of the nigga you were with, and two, video call his ass."

He nodded frantically, looking scared but slightly relieved. That would be short lived, of course, because he was still going to die.

After giving us the name of the person he was with, he FaceTimed him.

"Yo Bear, these niggas got me!" he panted into the phone with blood running down his face.

"Bear, is that you?" Sin teased, turning the camera around on himself since he was the one holding the phone. "Yo' man here is gonna die, and in a few days, you will too, after I catch up with you, nigga. Make sure you make plans and tell yo' niggas The Wolf Pack sends their regards!"

Bear hung up and Sin stuffed Dante's phone in his pocket.

"Time's up, nigga. We just needed yo' buddy's name."

Dante's bitch ass immediately began to cry as if that was going to stop us from killing his ass. He'd shot me and there was no way he got to live after that.

We began to drag Dante toward the cage I kept in the back of the property we were at. I called it the breeding grown because it was on a remote piece of land with sound barriers lining the perimeter. They weren't needed because there were no neighbors for miles but I had them just in case. It was the first piece of property I'd purchased after getting any type of money. I added all the extra shit when I got my pharmaceutical check.

"Ow!" I said, dropping Dante to the ground. I had the back of his shirt and was dragging him from the front, but the way he was kicking and carrying on, it was too much for me. I was still healing from where his hoe ass shot me at.

"Shoot that nigga again, Sin."

Sin pulled his gun from his side holster and fired a shot into Dante's arm.

"I told you nigga, that the second shot would be there."

The nigga was screaming at the top of his lungs. While he was in pure agony, I found the shit quite comical. The world was full of bad motherfuckers. I was fucked up and twisted, but I only did evil when evil was done to me. A nigga had to balance the scales. If a person did me dirty, I was going to do them filthy. I didn't give a damn who it was. I made it clear to people not to fuck with me. It was on them after they did.

After being shot a second time, he put up less of a fight. Sin and I drug him to the back of the house and into a large, closed-in shed. It was nearly the size of a small house and inside of it was a custom cage filled with a rare breed of imported gray wolves. You see, wolves were my thing. I got the nickname when I was a child and used to play outside. During that time, there had been a few rare wolf sightings. Me being a curious little fella, I often played outside in the woods in the back of my house out of boredom. One day, I found what appeared to be a puppy. Come to find out, it was a wolf. One that I insisted on feeding and keeping. My parents were against it, but decided to let me hold onto it. Of course, I eventually realized why that was. It was to teach me a lesson, because the first chance that little motherfucker got, it bit me. Despite that, I still took a liking to that particular animal and that became my nickname.

After I got my first large check, I ordered a batch of baby wolves and trained them to be vicious. I fed them meat and blood until they craved it. They'd been bred for shit like this. After quickly tossing Dante into the cage with them, I sat back and watched as they all rushed toward him and began mauling him. Dante's screams made my adrenaline rush.

While they bit, tore, and chewed, Sin and I continued to watch in awe. The only thing that broke me from my trance was the vibration of my phone. I pulled it out and looked at it. It was Cash. I glanced at Sin.

"I gotta take this," I told him nonchalantly.

I was talking as if I was getting up from watching a movie, and not watching a man be murdered.

"Wassup, Cash?" I asked her. I had walked out of the soundproof shed and was now standing outside.

"Wolf! It's my grandmother. She was rushed to the hospital."

I didn't even let her finish.

"I'm on my way to you."

Chapter 15
Cashmere "Cash" Ellis

Walking through the automatic doors of the emergency room, I couldn't help but feel guilty. My grandmother's health had been deteriorating and I knew firsthand how quickly things could go from bad to worse. That was the story of my fucking life. Wolf, of course, wouldn't allow me to blame myself. Right after he picked me up from the hotel, he sped as fast as he could back to Beetlesburg. The hospital had called me and told me that my grandmama had been rushed to the hospital after she hit her Life Alert key chain. Her oxygen levels had dipped to 5 percent and unfortunately, when she got to the hospital she was unconscious. She died shortly after.

"You've been living with her but let's be honest Cash, you and your siblings have been taking care of your grandma since y'all got here. She did her best but she's been sick. There's nothing you could have done to stop the inevitable, nothing at all. So don't let me hear you blaming yourself ever again."

My eyes blinked uncontrollably as I fought back the surge of tears that was coming.

"Okay," I managed to choke out. After a few minutes of being wrapped in Wolf's arms and curled against his chest. I was all cried out ...for the moment anyway. I had to figure out what I would do next. What my next move would be. I knew that my grandmama's time was going to come, I just didn't realize how soon it would be. I never thought that I'd be alone with no one. I'd never been alone before. Mentally I was lost, and I wasn't ready.

"Wolf, I-I can't stay in that house by myself. I've never been alone before."

"Okay, and you don't ever have to be. Let me put you up for a night or two. Take you somewhere you'll be nice and comfortable at."

I gave him a reluctant look.

"I'm not trying to rush or force you into anything. I just want to be there for you, so you don't have to be alone. You can stay with Fat Ma in my room, and I'll go to a hotel. Whatever will make you comfortable. She won't mind you crashing there for a night or two," he told me.

I shook my head no.

"No. I don't want her to have to get up at this time of night. I'll do the hotel."

"Okay."

I took a deep breath and then got up. The day had started off amazing but had ended horribly. When I stood to my feet, a wave of dizziness swept over me.

"You okay?" Wolf asked as I shook it off.

"Yeah." I grabbed his arm, and with his support, we left.

After we left from the hospital, I convinced Wolf to stop me home to get some clothes. He continuously told me that I didn't need anything and he would get me what I needed, but I insisted. He finally agreed after my persistence. I couldn't lie, I was in a daze. Wolf walked me into the house in fear that I would fall out. I was distraught but I was still aware enough to know that he gave himself a mini tour of my grandmama's place. My heart hurt too much to be embarrassed about anything. I was strictly focused on my pain. I grabbed what I could find that was clean, and left. The entire ride, I stared out the window and just took in the nothing that sat outside. I was so tired of Georgia as a whole. It had been horrible to my family, and I wanted to get out and go far away.

I ended up dozing off and when I woke up, I realized that Wolf had driven to a hotel in Atlanta. I could tell because of the tall buildings and bright lights, but I still asked.

"We in Atlanta?"

"Yeah," he replied with a nod. "I booked the hotel on the way here. Come on," he said.

I began loading up the small bag I had grabbed from the house after leaving the hospital.

"You can leave that shit," he said.

"What am I gonna wear?" I asked, still adjusting from my recent nap.

"Stop worrying about shit like that. I'll buy you new everything."

I hesitated but sat the bag back down. Wolf grabbed it and we began walking to the front door of the lobby. The St. Regis was the name of the hotel. The place was gorgeous with a fountain in the front. There were all kinds of beautiful cars parked in the parking lot. Foreign cars that I'd only seen on TV. The building itself looked like a grand mansion. I was now really beginning to understand the type of luxuries that Wolf's money could afford. And even though he offered to do things for me and took me along with him, I didn't want to get used to his lifestyle. It wasn't my reality, but I still allowed my eyes to widen and take it all in.

Right before we entered, Wolf tossed my bag in the trash. I

wanted to protest because those were my things, but I didn't say anything. After checking in, we headed up the elevator and checked into our suite. That too was just as beautiful as expected. The furniture was sleek and modern, and the view was breathtaking. For a moment, I wanted to twirl around like a little girl. I'd been poor all my life and moments like this were simply imagined in dreams.

"This is beautiful, Wolf. Thank you."

"You're welcome," he said.

After walking through the suite, I stood at the window and soaked up the city view. It was nice. A beautiful black sky with twinkling stars. My thoughts drifted to my grandmama. How I wished she could see what I saw. I wondered if she ever even saw anything like this. Then I wondered how she felt being all alone. Did she call for me? Did she suffer? Was she in more pain than she normally was? I began to cry but I tried to hide it. I guess Wolf noticed it, because he came up behind me, turned me around, and pulled me into his arms. I sobbed into his chest for several minutes while he occasionally kissed the top of my head and cheeks.

"I'm sorry," I finally said a few minutes later after pulling my head away from his body.

"Sorry for what? For being human?"

He pulled one arm from around my torso and used his hand to wipe away the tears from my face.

"Don't ever be sorry for showing emotion. Grieve completely. Love completely. And do your best to live completely."

I sighed, doing my best to absorb his message.

"Okay," I told him.

"Seriously. And I know you may be worried because she was all you feel you had, but I want you to know that you got me and I got you. You don't have to worry about nothing, you hear me."

I nodded.

He gave me an intense look and I looked away. Wolf's ass had me feeling a way I had never felt before. I believed he had me the way he said he did. Just the way he held me in his arms made me feel safe. I was falling for him and he knew it. I could see it in his eyes. The way he looked at me. He knew.

"Look at me," he said, lifting my chin so our eyes could meet.

I felt weak.

"You believe I gotchu?" he asked.

"Yes," I said.

My response came out in nearly a whisper as I struggled to breathe normally. My mental state had made me vulnerable.

"Good."

Wolf leaned in and gently pressed his lips against mine. To keep from losing my damn mind, I closed my eyes for a few seconds, eventually pulling away.

"I ain't no distraction, Cash. You'll see that soon enough though. But I know you're vulnerable and you're going through something. I won't take advantage of that. But just know."

He paused and then his signature white and gold grin flashed to his chocolate face.

"Know you can get this dick whenever you're ready."

I rolled my eyes but burst into laughter at the same time.

"I'll just hold you tonight if you can control yourself," he continued.

"I'll try," I replied.

My grandmama had been gone for a week and I was at mental capacity. I didn't know if I could handle anything else. It was more guilt than anything because I felt like I should have been there. I was always there. But because I went out on a fucking date, my grandmama basically transitioned alone. Wolf did his best to convince me that it wasn't my fault, but it was hard for my brain to accept that. He offered me everything he could think of to make shit easier for me. He gave me rides, encouraging words, and even offered to help me out financially. Of course, I refused. I knew he had a lot of money but I didn't want him thinking that was all I wanted. I was growing to care about Wolf and I refused to take from him what I felt I didn't need. Thankfully, my grandmama had a small policy that luckily was, by the grace of God, still active. She'd purchased it years back when she was still young and healthy. With all her health conditions, I was surprised they hadn't canceled it.

"You got anything else to do today?" Wolf asked.

We had been running around all day and had finally stopped to get something to eat. There wasn't a whole lot good to choose from in Beetlesburg, so we ended up going to get burgers and fries from Wendy's. Wolf wasn't big on McDonald's, but he'd fuck some Wendy's up.

"No. That was pretty much it."

I'd already been to the funeral home and arranged for her cremation. I didn't plan to have a funeral. She didn't really fuck with anyone in Beetlesburg. All her siblings were dead. I hadn't seen my uncle Otis, nor did I know how to get in touch with him. We'd never met her extended family, and I didn't feel like going through the embarrassment of trying to have a service for her and only three people show up. Me, Wolf, and Fat Ma. I wanted to get away from Beetlesburg the very first opportunity I got.

Wolf and I sat in silence, eating in the car for a little while, when a thought came to me.

"I actually do need to go back to the house. I gotta find my grandmama's deed."

"You gon' sell the place?"

"Yeah. If anyone even wants it. It's raggedy as fuck. I'd be thankful to even get five grand for it."

Wolf shrugged and continued to bite into his sandwich.

"Stay positive, babe. I'm sure someone will give you more for it."

Babe. He'd called me babe. And he said the shit like he truly meant it. I didn't know why the small words had me feeling some type of way, but they did. When I first met Wolf, he was impatient and at times a tad mean, but over the last couple weeks he had softened up. I remembered being unsure of what he wanted from me, and I was still unsure but for the first time, I did get the notion that he truly liked me. I just wasn't sure why. What the fuck did I offer, or could I offer, that another bitch couldn't?

"I'm trying to stay positive," I finally responded with a smile, shaking off all the thoughts of him I had swirling around in my head.

"It's just a lot," I continued.

"I know it is. That's why we're gonna take a little trip."

"A trip?" I eyed him as I shoved a few crinkled fries in my mouth and began to chew.

"You asking me or telling me?"

"Telling you."

I hated that he was so bossy but in a sense, I kind of liked it. I low-key liked being told what to do, and Wolf's dominant nature was actually very attractive.

Chapter 16
Ezekiel "Wolf" Griffin

I ended up flying Cash out to Miami, Florida, on a quick two-day vacation. It was so short because Fat Ma claimed she needed her back so she could work the front since Lou had been having health issues and was out sick. Cash had already been off for over a week due to her grandma's passing. I didn't like her working up in the store, but I wasn't going to say anything right away. She didn't need it anymore, but she liked to be independent, and Fat Ma relied on her.

Cash and I had grown super close since her people had passed away. I'd lost my mama and sister and Cheese's absence had been impactful mentally, but I'd never really lost anyone else I cared about. I tried to keep those special people to a minimum. I didn't do well with grief, and watching Cash go through it made me stop everything I was doing and tend to her.

I cared about her. A nigga even got warm and fuzzy feelings when I thought about her and when she was around. I liked it, so I kept her around as much as I could. I was a gangsta but thugs needed loved too. Until Cash completely trusted me, I was going to stick around a little bit. I wasn't staying in no bullshit-ass Beetlesburg, so I purchased the first home I could find that was close by, near the whities. It wasn't as big as I'd like it to be because I didn't plan for me and Cash to stay in it much, but it had a yard, a nice porch, and a couple big-ass bedrooms. It was actually 5,000 square feet. Small to me but grand to most.

Cash damn near fell out when she seen the shit. I could've sworn I saw her pinch and slap her own self a few times to make sure she wasn't dreaming. But as beautiful as it was, she was reluctant about moving in. She didn't want to be that close to me and have me feeling some type of way. Even though we'd kissed, she still wasn't ready for sex. I couldn't lie, I wanted her bad. For sure wanted to nail her ass to the cross. But I wanted her to be ready for a nigga.

Cash was simple but she was sexy. Her airy spirit, her beaming smile. Not only was she my dog, but she was my girl too. I never said it flat out, but she already knew what was up. I took her shopping for new clothes, I started getting her hair and nails done, and I took her greedy ass out to eat damn near every night. She wasn't used to good food, so she was living it up. I even started picking her up in the Bentley when I noticed some little corny-ass nigga lurking around out the blue. When I asked her who it was she said it was some young, lame-ass nigga named Jermaine. He looked like he had a thang for her and after inquiring, Cash admitted that she let the nigga eat her pussy. That shit didn't sit well with me. I hadn't even touched my bitch, and that nigga had.

Motherfuckers were hating, especially the niggas. Buck and Johntay wanted to know how I'd managed to snatch her ass up that quickly. Of course, I told them niggas to mind their fucking business. What was understood damn sure didn't need to be explained to nobody. Cash and I had a history further than anyone could ever imagine. Our lives had become intertwined over ten years ago. I still hadn't told Cash that my pops was part of the robbery that killed her parents, and I wasn't sure that I ever would. As we grew closer, Fat Ma kept telling me that I should tell her. I just wasn't sure how she would take it, and I was to the point where I didn't want to lose her before I truly had her.

I had other bitches fucking and sucking on me when I went back and forth to Atlanta to meet up with my team and handle some business, but I wanted Cash. For now, I had her sitting pretty in her own little castle, like the princess she was. But I had bigger shit planned for her. She'd gotten just a crumb of what I had in store for her. Just a speck of the good life that was waiting for her. I just needed a little more time to make sure that she was everything I thought she was. Once I found that out, I was going to make her love me. And then and *only* then would she know who Wolf truly was.

Chapter 17
Satin Ellis

I remembered the days I hated my period because I couldn't afford to buy a pad to sit under my ass. Now I was thankful anytime blood ran from my body because that meant it would finally get a break. For the last two years, Zander had us fucking and sucking every single day. In his eyes, there was always money to be made. There'd been times I'd fuck ten niggas in a day. The only time my coochie got a break was when it was that time of month.

I'd been pregnant three times by Chop and once by Zander. The niggas not only made money off of us, but they also used us like their personal sex slaves. Whatever they wanted to try, they used us to make their dreams and fantasies come true. If they wanted their ass ate for the first time, guess who made that happen? Wanted their dicks and balls sucked, we did that too.

There wasn't a part of their bodies that we hadn't touched and their wish was our fucking command.

We were walking zombies most days. High off drugs to make the shit we endured daily more manageable. I enjoyed the poison they fed to us day in and day out simply because it made tolerating that shit easier.

There were no landlines in the rooms or houses that we occupied. We had no cellphones and using force, they kept us captive and under their control. In the beginning, we used to fight every chance we could to get away. However, the beatings got worse and worse. It had become our norm. I'd been pistol whipped several times, strangled with shoestrings, hit with objects. I'd even had the soles of my feet burned with a lighter.

Every beating I took caused my spirit to weaken and weaken. There was no escaping. I was a possession. Someone's property. It had been that way so long, I stopped resisting. I stopped putting up a fight. In a weird way, I'd formed a bond with my captors. It was easier to get along with them than to try and fight them. It became a psychological thing.

Every now and then they'd bring a few new young girls in. But their spirits hadn't been broken yet and even when they did get away, there was usually no retribution or arrests made. We were violated daily and unless it was a big case that made the news, nobody gave a fuck.

I used to want to kill myself but after a while, I started to use my thoughts to figure out how to get away. For a long time, I didn't realize how much power pussy possessed. I'd go in my room, fuck, and repeat. We were told not to talk. Not to make a connection. But just like in school and growing up, being told what we could and couldn't do, we never listened. I'd never really do much talking if it was my first time with a man. I didn't want to say much because it could be my last time with him. Why the fuck would I break down my sad ass life story to a stranger? To a nigga that didn't give a fuck. To a nigga that was only worried about busting a nut in me or on me.

It wasn't until I started getting the regulars that I started to act on the ideas that were swirling around in my head. Talk to them. Ask them questions. Those starts would sit in my head session after session. They were coming back for a reason. I wanted to find out why. *Was it that my pussy was good? Did they like me as a person?* Then I started to wonder, what if they did like me as a person? I wanted to get out. *Would they help me?* The average male that paid for pussy like ours, when I say like ours, I meant questionable pussy. Some of us were so fucking young that it was no way we were doing that shit on our own will. Them motherfuckers knew that. They just didn't care.

The first few trick niggas that I learned was low-key feeling me was the first time I tried to see how far my pussy would take me. I had a shot of liquid courage in me, and I was so high off drugs that I fell into the role of seductress. *What will you do with no regards to the consequences?* It started off small. Sneak me in some candy. Some extra money. Break me off outside of what you already paid. They passed with flying colors. After testing them on a small scale, I went big and tested them on a larger scale. I told them what was really up. Told them that I had basically been kidnapped and sex trafficked. I needed their help to escape. To get out of there and get my life back. Would they help me?

The first bitch-ass nigga flat out refused. He was shook and didn't want any parts. Seduction mission failed. The second one was apprehensive but willing as long as we could do it safely. However, the catch was he would help me with the exception that we be together. It was then that I knew pussy was power. Your situation can be manipulated or swayed if you used it correctly.

Men were easy like that. And when you wanted what you wanted, you made shit simple by leveraging. If I wanted to get into a party but was being denied entry, a little head was a fair exchange. I got what I needed accomplished. That was usual shit. Zander would send us in a club and we were told that we'd better get in no matter what to squeeze some money out of it. We did what we had to do.

Going back to the nigga that agreed to help me. When they figured out he was trying to help me escape, they pistol whipped and shot him dead. But that didn't stop me from trying again. The second trick that tried to help me got beaten up and then, of course, stopped coming. I didn't know if he was alive or dead, but from the sick-ass jokes that the niggas would crack in there, I knew he was probably dead in a shallow-ass grave somewhere. Those niggas didn't give a fuck about life and somewhere along the way, I stopped caring as well. They had the ability to snatch my life from me at any time and I was ashamed to say, I didn't even care. There were times I wanted to die. We weren't living. We were waking up and dying over and over again. Drugs made me feel better and helped me escape.

This life was unfortunately my norm. I thought about my sister, brother, and grandma all the time. I wondered what they were doing and what they were up to. I wondered if they missed me or had searched for me. I prayed that one day I would see them again. But until that day came, all I could do was focus on getting through each day.

The bitter night air gnawed at my fingertips and cheeks, producing a dull ache. It was the dead of December. I wasn't sure what day. All I knew was November had passed and a lot of the houses we passed had Christmas lights and decor up. The radio stations had holiday songs in heavy rotation. I'd heard Mariah Carey's "All I Want for Christmas" a million times, and I damn near could recite Eartha Kitt's "Santa Baby"

word for word. I loved Christmas and even though we stopped getting anything after our folks died, they'd left a lasting impact on our souls about how Christmas was supposed to feel.

I wasn't certain where we were at, but I did know that we were a long way from home and somewhere in Georgia. We moved around a lot and played the truck stops heavily during retail season or peak shopping season. Since Christmas was nearing, the truck stops were filled and bustling with activity. Lonely truckers on the road for days and weeks at a time were our main source of income in the winter. Them niggas had us up and down the East Coast selling pussy. From as far north as New York and as far south as Florida. Buffalo, Pittsburg, Richmond, Miami.

My eyes quickly scanned the bleak scene around me and then into the store. Two workers and a parking lot full of truckers. Chop shot me a look as if to say, "I know what you're up to. Don't get no fuckin' ideas." They knew the first chance I got, I would run. I'd bolted off on they ass several times at different truck stops. Over time, I learned that I wouldn't get far. They took us to remote truck stops just for that reason. So, if we ran, there would be nowhere to go. Nothing but highway where they'd find us quickly. The gas stations and travel lodges had posters everywhere about seeing and reporting human trafficking, and the motherfuckers working the stores and frequenting the stores did absolutely nothing to help us. They were scared just like we were, and they had every reason to be.

Our abductors weren't Albanian or Russian-speaking white men. A lot of these men were a part of gangs. I'm talking, teams of pimps and criminals. Some white. Think biker guys with big arms and tattoos. Some black. Picture a couple hood niggas from Atlanta with Dracos in the trunk. That's the type of danger women like us were faced to live and deal with on a day-to-day basis. Scared of what will happen if we fight back, run, or try and tell someone. Trust me, I'd tried it all. The fighting back got me beat and drug across the floor so hard, my hair was ripped out my head. The running got me kicked, punched, and the soles of my feet burned. Imagine still having to get on your knees and suck dick with blisters on the bottom of your feet. Or imagine being bent over doggy style standing on tippy toes with blisters. I couldn't complain out of fear of being beat. After a while, I learned if you can't beat them, join them. I understood why they choose that business. Sex was lucrative.

"What the fuck y'all waiting on?" Chop's fat ass barked out.

I looked at him and did my best to hide the disgust that threatened to surface on my face. I never liked Chop. I actually despised him. He knew it and was extra mean and spiteful every chance he got. That, unfortunately ,was often. Even though I hated his guts, he still made it his business to fuck me several times a week and the other times, he forced me to suck his dick or whatever he wanted sucked at the time. Dick, fingers, shit ... his disgusting ass even had me lapping at his toes a few times. The one time I refused one of his disgusting requests, I found myself waking up after being knocked out cold. Not only that, but when I came to, my entire body had been doused with water and I was naked. Even in my unconscious state, Chop chose to violate me. I had his semen smeared all on my face and blood trickling down my thigh where he had fucked me viciously. With blood on the barrel of the Glock he had nearby, I had a feeling he'd used that.

I did my best to stay away from him, but that only fueled him. The more I rejected him, the more violent he became. So, I stopped rejecting him.

"What, you bitches deaf or something?" Chop continued to

argue. "Coffee, you take the left side, and Cream, you take the right."

Those were our code names. We never went by our real names. Ever. I was Coffee because of my deep-chocolate complexion and Amber was Cream because of her fair skin.

"We on it, Papa," I said to Chop with little emotion.

Being held against your will and forced to sell pussy hardened you. A bitch had to remain emotionless to survive. Life was hard as fuck and downright terrible. If I let my emotions get the best of me, I'd be a dead bitch because taking my own life would be overwhelmingly tempting.

"I'm so sick of this shit," Amber mumbled just loud enough for me to hear.

Her words came out bitterly and the look on her face was somber. I knew that something was going on in her brain that she couldn't quite explain. She'd been quiet, dark, and sad. It was new since from the beginning of our horrible experience, she was the one who kept us together. She was the one who made us look on the bright side of things no matter how fucked up our situation was. She'd still sing and try to crack jokes to keep our spirits lifted the entire two years. However, that all changed when she suffered her very first miscarriage.

"We're gonna be fine girl, let's just get this shit over with and then we can get back to the hotel."

Amber didn't respond. She took her side of the lot and then I took mine. We lived a fucked-up life but the way I saw it, at least we were still living.

* * *

"You okay?" I asked Amber when we got back into the hotel room and were preparing to shower.

Her fair skin seemed a little paler than normal. She had a

thin film of sweat on her head and she was moving around very slowly. Her steps were methodic, and she was using her hand to balance her weight against things. "I'm fine," she mumbled before stumbling against the dresser.

"You're not fine. Sit down somewhere. I'll grab a rag and some water for you to drink." I grabbed her arm and helped her sit on the bed. She immediately laid down. I walked off into the bathroom to wet a rag and grab her some tap water out of the faucet. My eyes quickly scanned the bathroom for one of those small, clear cups individually wrapped in plastic. I found one in the corner of the sink. Opening it, I quickly filled it with some room temperature water before soaking and wringing out a rag to throw over her head. My girl was sick and was probably coming down with something. She needed some rest and if I had to pick up the slack by fucking her share of niggas, then I would.

"What the fuck?" I yelled when I bent the corner and saw Amber convulsing and foaming at the mouth.

It looked like she was having a seizure. Her eyes were half open, her arms flailed around wildly, and thick, white foam ran from the side of her mouth. I dropped the rag and cup of water that I was holding and ran over to her. Her eyes were rolling back but all of a sudden, they closed.

"Amber baby, wake up!" I cried.

I rolled her over on her stomach so she wouldn't choke and then ran over to the phone and dialed 911. Amber was still foaming and shaking until she suddenly stopped moving. I screamed for help at the top of my lungs.

When the ambulance arrived, the paramedics acted quickly, recognizing the signs of an overdose. Fear and guilt washed over me; I didn't realize she had taken something. They did everything in their power to reverse the overdose, but despite their efforts, Amber's condition remained critical.

As the paramedics worked on Amber, I knew I needed to find help. I ran to the motel rooms down the hall, where our pimps, Chop and Zander, were staying. I couldn't bear the weight of this alone. They rushed back with me, and seeing Amber's condition, their anger momentarily replaced with concern. As the ambulance took Amber away, their emotions turned toward me, blaming me for the situation. They lashed out, beating me, even though it wasn't my fault.

After the ambulance left, I found myself in a corner, tears streaming down my face, wailing in pain and regret. I wished I had the courage to take my life too, but deep down, I knew I couldn't let this darkness consume me. Amber needed me now more than ever.

I made a vow to get help for both of us, to leave this life behind, and to never let another person I care about suffer like this. The pain and heartache seemed unbearable, but I knew I had to fight for Amber and myself, no matter how hard the road ahead would be.

Chapter 18
Cashmere "Cash" Ellis

I glanced at the clock on the wall. Even though it was old and beginning to fade a little, I could still make out the time: 7:35. I had twenty-five minutes left before I could close the store, but I was ready to go like yesterday. Fat Ma was already in the back putting away cash and doing some paperwork while I was pouring cleaner into a mop bucket and preparing to run some water so I could mop the floor.

The day had been very busy. It was the first of the month and it fell on a Friday. That meant the people whose check normally came on the third got it early because their check day fell on a weekend. Not only that, but welfare checks and food stamps had dropped. Even though Fat Ma's store didn't cash checks, she took food stamps, sold cigarettes, and sold female staples like cheap hair weave, knockoff bags, and paper-thin outfits. Folks had extra money to spend so they were in and out of the store spending a few dollars on what they wanted and the rest on what they needed to get them through the month.

As the only cashier working because Lou was still sick, I had a line from the front of the store damn near to the back of the store most of the day. I had so much shit to do before I could leave, I didn't even want to think about it. I'd already swept, but I still had to mop, lock the doors, restock put backs, and clean the fryer. Normally none of these things bothered me but after meeting Wolf, I wanted to get out of there as fast as I could. Wolf would text and call me in the morning, and we would hang out during the day. There was always something to do when we got together. Always somewhere to explore. I pushed the door closed, pushed the key in the slot, and was about to turn the lock when the door basically shattered in my face. Two males rushed toward me with black bandannas tied on their face. The scarves covered everything but their eyes while the hats they wore hid their heads.

When the glass shattered, I instinctively released the lock while the men rushed inside, the first one knocking me to the ground. He stood over top of me with a baseball bat while the other held a gun. The one carrying the firearm began screaming, "Where's the fucking money!"

The eerie feeling of déjà vu crept over me, making me instantly nauseous. My energy levels dropped to zero and as I sat on the floor, my pitiful life flashing slowly before my eyes.

"Please," I said weakly to the man still standing over top of me.

He had the baseball cocked back like he was ready to bash my head in. There was nothing left to do but try and reason with him. But even though my lips had parted to speak, nothing came out. Fear had paralyzed my vocal cords.

"Where the money at, bitch?" he asked me, just as I heard Fat Ma scream from the back of the store. Hearing her voice caused something to ignite inside of me. Words began to flow from my trembling lips.

"The safe is in the back office under the desk. Code is 10, 22, 5."

Fat Ma had already programmed me on what to do in a robbery. We were in a country ass town, but it was still the hood. Niggas and bitches were poor, and ghetto and robbery was something we always had to be prepared for. People loved and respected Fat Ma in the hood, but that alone wasn't enough to stop a motherfucker from robbing her.

"Got it, nigga! Come back and empty this shit out!" the gun-wielding man yelled out excitedly.

The man carrying the baseball bat took off running to the back of the store where Fat Ma was opening the safe. He was moving so quickly that he knocked over a three-tier fruit stand and a couple of racks. With him no longer hovering above me menacingly, I used that as my opportunity to call for help.

Despite all the glass all over the floor, I used my palms to get up, ignoring the pain from the cuts the tiny shards of glass were leaving behind.

"Bitch, where the fuck you think you're going?"

They had switched places. The man toting the gun had come to the front and the man with the bat was now in the back with Fat Ma. My eyes watched his hand carefully as that paralyzing fear returned. My eyes scanned his physique discreetly. I knew him. His voice had intentionally deepened but I knew him.

"You don't fuckin' move 'til I say so."

He unexpectedly reached out and yanked me back to the ground by my hair and began to drag me into a corner.

I immediately began screaming at the top of my lungs.

"Get the fuck off me!"

"Bitch, shut up. While I'm here, I'ma get some of this little pussy."

I now recognized who it was.

"Jermaine, please!" I cried, squirming underneath his weight.

He now had me toward the back of the store on the side of an aisle. Rice and vegetables lined the shelves while I flailed, kicked, and screamed.

"Didn't I say shut the fuck up!" He slapped me across the face so hard that I saw stars.

"And don't say my fuckin' name again!"

Tears rolled out my eyes and I stopped fighting for a second. But only for a second. When I realized what his ass was about to do, a surge of adrenaline and strength roared through my body.

"You already let me taste that pussy. Now you gon' let me feel it."

I had on a thin pair of tights and a t-shirt. Jermaine grabbed the waistband of my leggings and snatched them down, exposing a third of my thigh.

"Please, no!" I wailed desperately as I realized his sick, barbaric ass was really about to rape me.

"Shut the fuck up! You 'bout to give that pussy up!"

Through his mask, I could see the passion and fury in his eyes. The nigga was really about to rape me! My heart thumped against my chest and fear choked me to the point that I could barely breathe. I felt overwhelmed and lightheaded, like I was in a fog and slipping away from reality. While I felt the urge to pass out, Jermaine used his weight to hold down my legs.

"Ewww, what the fuck!" Jermaine yelled after forcing his hands into my panties.

He snatched his hand back and finally looked down.

"You nasty bitch!" he yelled after drawing his hand back and seeing that it was damp.

That old habit that I could never seem to shake had returned. Terrified by Jermaine's actions, I had pissed on myself. But I guess it was just my luck, because Jermaine shoved my legs to the side in disgust and jumped from off top of me.

"Let's go, nigga!" he yelled to the back.

A few seconds later, the other masked guy that came in with Jermaine ran out the back with a small bag of cash.

"Jackpot, nigga!" he yelled out as they dashed out the store.

While I sat on the floor crying, bleeding, and pissy, Fat Ma emerged from the back with her telephone in her hand. She was calling 911.

"I'll call Wolf," I said, my lip trembling.

I was still trying to process what had just happened, and I almost had the urge to piss myself again as my mind attempted to replay it.

"Don't," she said sternly.

"Why? We need him. You think they'll be back? It's not safe?" I asked, my eyes widening.

"Honey, we're okay. We're safe. They, on the other hand, are not."

Chapter 19
Ezekiel "Wolf" Griffin

"What happened?" I asked Cash, storming into the store.

Just looking at the shattered front door had my blood boiling. I wanted to know who, what, and when, and I wanted to know like yesterday.

Fat Ma had called me and told me that the store had been robbed nearly an hour ago. A whole fucking hour! I was pissed. I wanted to know why she hadn't called me as soon as it happened. I needed answers, and I knew that Fat Ma was going to dumb down what happened because that was the type of shit she did. She already knew what type of nigga I was and how I was coming. She wouldn't want me to get into any trouble, but trouble had literally came through the front door. It was too late for that. So, instead of playing games with Fat Ma, I figured I would get everything I needed out of Cash before she could intervene.

"Is she still being questioned?" I asked the two police that were standing and talking to Cash.

I wanted them to wrap that shit up so I could get to the bottom of what happened.

"Actually, no. She's free to go."

Cash looked at me through wide, helpless eyes. She was scared and I didn't like that. It actually pissed me off more. People were about to die. I grabbed her arm gently and walked her out. Fat Ma was near the front counter, talking to another officer. I wanted to get Cash to myself.

"Come outside with me."

I led her outside and she looked confused when we got out there.

"Who's that?" she asked.

Her eyes landed on the powder blue Ferrari that was parked against the curb a few feet behind mine. As soon as I heard that Fat Ma's had been robbed, I called Sin to meet me in Beetlesburg. It took forty-five minutes to get there from Atlanta, but it took him thirty.

"My homie, but right now ain't the time for the meet and greet. I need to ask you some questions and I need you to answer them quickly and be completely honest with me, okay," I told her. I looked dead in her eyes to let her know that I was serious. Her look in response was one of nervousness.

"Who came in the store?"

She folded her arms into her chest and looked down at the ground.

"My ex, Jermaine."

"Who else?"

"I don't know who the other guy was. He had on a mask, and I didn't recognize his voice."

"How did you know it was Jermaine?"

"His voice. At first I wasn't sure, but I knew for sure when he tried to rape me. But he stopped when..." Her voice trailed off, but that was all I needed anyway.

"That's all I needed, babe. You stay with Fat Ma tonight. I'll pick you up in the morning."

"Wait. What? You're not coming home?"

"No. I got something to handle. Go back inside."

* * *

I had four cars behind me. Before Sin and I left Fat Ma's, I made one phone call to summon the pack. The average boss like me would have sent niggas to get at his ass, but I wasn't the average boss. I rolled straight up to that nigga's house personally. At first I rolled up to the little neighborhood hang-out spot where I knew Buck and Johntay would be. They knew somebody, that knew somebody, and it didn't take long before I had Jermaine's direct address.

My face was calm, but my heart was filled with rage. I'd always been a peaceful nigga till someone fucked with me or someone I loved. Jermaine and the nigga he was with would learn that the hard way. They were going to die, and it was all because they didn't know any better.

"Clear the block," I told Sin as I hopped out the passenger side of his Ferrari. I'd left my Bentley at the crib. When shit was done and over, Sin and the crew would go back to Atlanta. I wasn't worried about any witnesses because by the time I got finished, motherfuckers would be too scared to breathe, let alone talk.

Several of my soldiers took off and began waving their automatic weapons around at any nosy motherfucker that thought they wanted to be a part of what was about to take place.

Jermaine didn't come out, but I saw the blinds move. I knew for a fact that his pussy ass was in the house, and I was about to bring him out.

"Bring his ass out!" I yelled, and they knew that was their cue to go inside and get him.

I didn't give a fuck what that nigga had inside his crib. Whatever he had was no match for what was about to go up in that bitch. With the word to go, about five of my people ran up to the house and shot the door off the hinges. I didn't come to play. I went to the extreme. My team knew it and Beetlesburg was about to be reminded of that shit.

"Shut up, pussy!" one of my young niggas yelled as he walked Jermaine out the house with a Draco to his back.

"Please, it wasn't my idea."

The bitch-ass nigga was crying. And had the nerve to use those same trembling ass lips on my bitch.

I eyed him. Scrawny, nappy-headed ass nigga. What the fuck was Cash thinking?

"Bag his ass up," I said as soon as he got close to me.

Sin snatched a black garbage bag out his pocket and the bitch nigga really started wailing.

"Should've thought about that shit before you ran up in that sto' and tried to take money and pussy."

"Oh, this nigga a rapist?" Sin asked.

"Tried. So, you know what that mean, right?" My eyes twinkled with sin.

"We gon' have some fun with this nigga?"

"Oh yeah," I said sinisterly.

"Maybe we'll let the wolves rip him a new asshole?" Sin laughed. "Open the trunk!" he yelled to the homies.

Jermaine wasn't getting up in the Ferrari. My team had come down in a couple Chargers. We used them as mini hearses. If we put a nigga in the back of one, they weren't going to ever been seen again alive.

"Where we taking him?" Sin asked me after they'd tossed Jermaine into the back and prepared to leave.

"Breeding grounds," I said.

"He food?"

"Yeah, but I also got something special for him."

"You's a crazy nigga."

"You too, nigga," I laughed.

* * *

I wound up torturing Jermaine for a few hours just because he deserved it. The same dick he used to try and rape my shawty, I cut that motherfucker off. And not only did I cut it off, but I chopped it up and then put it in my food processor. I fed some to him and the rest to the wolves. Of course, that weak ass nigga couldn't keep his own dick down, but the wolves loved it. Imagine this nigga crying his fucking eyes out while they scarfed his shit down.

I wasn't worried about Jermaine bleeding to death because after cutting off his dick, I cauterized it with fire from a blow torch. My intention was to stop the bleeding and keep him alive long enough to have some more fun with him. That fun consisted of cutting off that nigga's lips too. Just because I felt like being petty. They'd been on my bitch, and I didn't like that, so they had to go. I sealed that wound with fire as well. Imagine the screams that came from his ass when that blow torch hit his face.

When it was all said and done, Jermaine was barely clinging to life and I was tired and bored. So, I tossed his ass in the cage and let my wolves finish him off for dinner.

Sin was there with me but only for the first few minutes. As soon as he realized I was cutting off that nigga's dick, he took off. Clown ass nigga talking 'bout he couldn't support that form of punishment. I can't lie, I got a good laugh off his ass. It was some cruel shit, but the way my brain was set up, when I had a vision for a nigga's death, it was going to happen that way.

When I was done with Jermaine, I went in, took a shower, and headed back to Beetlesburg to pick up Cash, just like I'd promised her.

Chapter 20
Cashmere "Cash" Ellis

After Jermaine disappeared, there wasn't a nigga in Beetlesburg that would say shit to me crazy. Everyone was showing me and Fat Ma the utmost respect. Fat Mama was already respected but once folks around there found out that her grandson was a crazy ass, Draco-toting goon from Atlanta, they damn near treated her with the respect of a queen. And it wasn't just Wolf that had folks shook, it was the crazy niggas he brought with him. They'd come into the city so quickly and instilled fear that no one wanted to feel again. Everybody knew that Wolf wasn't to be fucked with and they didn't want to ever be reminded of it again.

The situation actually hurt Fat Ma's business, especially because Wolf insisted on sitting his ass up at the store every day, all day. Even when she told him that sales were down, he still posted his Bentley out the front for everyone to see. It got so bad that she let me go and although I was pissed about it, Wolf seemed to be happy. That didn't sit well with me because I'd told him that I wanted to make sure I had me all the way together before I took things further. He thought that was stupid since we weren't just friends. We were already together 24/7 and already boyfriend and girlfriend. He was my nigga, and I was his bitch, as Wolf liked to call it. I didn't like the terms, but he swore he wasn't being disrespectful, so I just went with it.

Wolf wanted us to be connected in more ways than just mentally. To be honest, I was scared. Scared that I would be inadequate and scared that if he wasn't satisfied, he would leave me. Without my job, I was even more terrified. Wolf could always send me home, and how the hell would I pay bills and support myself? My head started fucking with me and I got depressed. Wolf noticed and asked me what I wanted and needed. I wanted security and even though he made promises to take care of me, it wasn't enough. My mama and daddy loved me, but they'd been snatched away and couldn't take care of me. If anything, I would have believed those words coming from their mouths before anyone else's. It wasn't enough for someone to take care of me, I had to take care of myself.

A few weeks later, Wolf surprised me with another trip to Atlanta. Even though I acted happy, I wasn't really thrilled because at this point, we were going to Atlanta so much. Nevertheless, that changed when he pulled up to a dark-brown brick building in what looked like the industrial section of the city.

"What's this place?" I asked, looking uninterested.

"Guess."

I sighed. I wasn't in a bad mood or anything. I was just a little tired from the ride.

"I don't know, Wolf. Just tell me. A store. We going shopping?" I asked, forcing a smile.

"Na. It's Le Fashion Lab."

I looked at him in confusion.

"Le Fashion Lab?" I repeated.

"Yeah. I've been paying attention. I noticed you like clothes but you like making your own more than you like buying them. This place is not only gonna teach you how to sew better but they're also going to teach you other skills just in case that's something you may want to do as a career. You know. Make clothes and shit."

I sat silently for a minute. Wolf could be so thoughtful at times. I went to speak but he cut me off.

"You don't have to go if you don't want. I paid the tuition already. If you decide to go, you're good and if you don't, we'll just donate that shit to someone else."

An overwhelming sense of gratitude came over me. It was things like this that made me care about him even more.

"Thank you, babe! Thank you!" I told him, calling him what he'd been calling me lately.

"We got the crib in Beetlesburg, but I figured to make it easy on you, we'll grab something right here in Atlanta. That way you'll be closer. I want you to be happy and I want you to be evolving like you want and not distracted."

An even bigger smile crept up on the side of my face. He always had to throw some slick shit up in his comment, but I knew he meant well, and I was thankful. I threw my arms around his neck and kissed him, but this time deeply, slipping my tongue in his mouth. I'd kissed both Jermaine and Wolf plenty of times. But with Wolf I felt a spark. I enjoyed it. I'd been saving myself because of my circumstances, but sitting there with Wolf and thinking about all the good that he'd brought to my life and value he added, I realized I no longer had to. I was going to make love to Wolf, or he was going to make love to me rather. It was going down and I was going to enjoy every moment of it.

* * *

Later that evening, I found myself standing in the middle of the bedroom Wolf and I shared. My heart was racing like a freight train. Wolf had been so patient and caring, helping me become a better version of myself. But now, I couldn't deny the feelings that were bubbling up inside me. I was eager to take our relationship to the next level, to make love to him, but my nerves were playing tricks on me.

Wolf entered the room with that warm smile of his, his eyes filled with tenderness as he looked at me. He noticed my unease, and without a word, he wrapped his arms around me, pulling me close in a reassuring embrace.

"You're beautiful, you know that?" he said softly, his breath tickling my ear. "And I'm not just talking about the outside, Cash. Your heart, your soul, everything about you is beautiful."

I blushed, feeling a mix of embarrassment and joy.

"Thank you. You've been so amazing to me, and I want to show you how much you mean to me," I confessed, my voice barely above a whisper.

He kissed my forehead gently, his touch sending shivers down my spine.

"We don't have to rush anything, Cash. I want you to be sure, and I want this to be special for you," he said, his voice full of understanding.

I looked up at him, my eyes locking with his.

"I am sure. I want this. I'm ready," I replied, trying to convey my sincerity.

He cupped my face in his hands and kissed me softly, his lips caressing mine in a tender dance. I felt my nervousness begin to fade away, replaced by a growing desire to be closer to him.

Slowly, he led me to bed, our fingers entwined. He kissed my neck and my body felt like it was about to give way. Like I could just crumble to the floor. I lay down on my back as Wolf moved slowly and deliberately. He told me that he was going to take his time with me the first round. That he would be gentle. And he was. Climbing on top of me, he began to kiss me slowly. He started with warm, gentle, wet kisses to my cheeks and then went further down. He kissed my collarbone and then my breasts, taking each one in his mouth and being attentive with them. My head turned from side to side as I could feel my mound moisten. I had never desired anyone as much as I did him.

Wolf continued to make his way down my body. He kissed my stomach and then dipped his tongue into my belly button. I shivered as his tongue swirled. By the time he had my legs in his arms and had parted my legs, I thought I was going to pass the fuck out. He dove his tongue in my pussy, and I fucking lost it. Jermaine hadn't made me feel this good and I was damn near crawling up the bed. My hands went from gripping the sheets to my sides to rubbing the back of his head furiously, to pushing it deeper. I moaned loudly as my eyes rolled to the back of my head and my knees buckled in his arms. That didn't stop him. He continued to lick, slurp, and occasionally use his fingers to stroke my mound and folds.

A few seconds later I was coming in his mouth as he still continued to lick.

"Baby, stop," I begged, when I felt like I couldn't take any more.

What had felt magnificent was now slightly overwhelming to my tender pussy. Wolf pulled his head from between my legs and smiled. His face was wet and it made him even more sexy. I rubbed his chest as he got up and pushed my legs apart farther with his own legs.

"You ready?" he asked.

I nodded. Although I was still nervous as hell, I was drunk off ecstasy. I had never felt that good in my life. Wolf leaned down and kissed my lips, sharing my juices with me. For some reason, it didn't even gross me out. My tongue intertwined with his, eagerly receiving my own nectar.

As Wolf kissed me, he shocked me by easing his manhood inside of me. I gasped as he felt like he was tearing through my fucking insides. In the movies, the bitches acted like fucking was the best thing they'd ever done, but this shit hurt like hell.

"Ahhhhhhh," I cried out.

"Shhhh, baby. Relax," he hushed me, thrusting gently to allow my tunnel to adjust to his girth and length. "Damn, you feel so good, baby. I promise it won't hurt long. Just relax."

I took a deep breath and did what he said. Wolf made sure I was comfortable, his every move gentle and considerate. There was no pressure, no rush, just two souls on the verge of something beautiful.

"You feel so good," he murmured against my ear, his warm breath sending shivers down my spine. "Just let go and trust me."

With every moment that passed, my nerves transformed into passion. I surrendered to him, to us, and it was more magical than I had ever imagined. Wolf made me feel loved, cherished, and desired, and all my worries vanished in his embrace.

In that intimate space, we found a deeper connection, one that went beyond physical pleasure. It was a meeting of hearts and souls, a culmination of the love and care we had shared over time.

Just as I was truly beginning to enjoy it and even digging my fingers into his ass cheeks, Wolf pulled himself out of me abruptly and held his dick, cumming into his hand.

"Shit," he said.

I lay there smiling, spent and breathless. The experience itself was beautiful. When he was done, Wolf got up and asked me to shower with him, where we washed off and he held me. I couldn't lie, at that moment, I felt closer to him. Actually, closer to anyone than I ever had.

After we showered, we got back into bed. The sheets were wet but Wolf said, 'fuck it.' We curled up together, right in our own juices. As we lay together, our bodies intertwined, my nervousness resurfaced. But Wolf was there, whispering sweet words of encouragement and showering me with affection. His touch was electrifying, igniting a fire within me that I had never felt before.

As the night faded away, we lay wrapped in each other's arms, basking in the afterglow of our newfound intimacy. I knew that my nerves had been worth it, and that I had found someone truly special in Wolf—a man who had helped me heal and grow, and who I couldn't wait to share my life with, one intimate moment at a time.

Since I had a lot of spare time and trips to Atlanta were getting old, I decided to start dropping in on Fat Ma. Since Wolf and I were an item, she was basically my family. I loved her like she was an additional grandmother. Store sales were picking back up, but they still weren't as strong as they used to be so Fat Ma was closing early. That meant she too had some extra time on her hands. During that time, we played cards, she taught me how to cook, and she took it upon herself to stop by and teach me how to clean properly. After coming by a few times and I had too many dishes in the sink and crumbs on the floor, she told me her grandson wasn't living in no dirty house and she was gon' get me together. And that she had.

"I need you to do something for me," Fat Ma said to me one

day while I was at her house learning how to bake cookies from scratch.

"What's that?"

"I need you to talk to Wolf about making amends with his daddy."

I stopped forming the dough into balls and stared at her from across the kitchen counter.

"You mean because of what happened to his mom?" I asked curiously.

"Yes. His father's health is declining, and I'd really like them to work out their differences. He loves you."

"How do you know?" I asked, my eyes lighting up as I got off topic.

"Stay focused, gal!" Fat Ma laughed. "Just talk to him. Life is too short."

She was right. It was. I'd never even seen Wolf and his father in the same room together. They way he spoke about him, he couldn't seem to stand him. Wolf said he was robbing people, and someone came after him, but he also said he was doing it to get cancer meds. I found that noble. Not something to be punished for. Sure, it ended badly, but he was already punishing himself. Wolf's father drank so much he had aged himself. He looked like he could've been Fat Ma's brother instead of her son. He stayed in the basement 24/7 and only came out to go get beer. Other times, Fat Ma would run him food downstairs and she would even wash his clothes. Out of boredom, I'd got in the habit of running down there as well to see what he needed, and during that time we'd made small talk. He was actually a friendly guy that spoke like he had some sense, although his words were slurred from alcohol.

Chapter 21
Ezekiel "Wolf" Griffin

"Why is he here, Cash?"

My voice seemed to roar through the living room, seemingly startling her because she jumped.

"Why the hell are you yelling!" she asked, her eyes round as fifty-cent pieces. "You scared the shit out of me."

Her palm still covered her chest.

"Why the fuck is he here?" I asked again. This time lower and through gritted teeth.

"Who? Your father?"

Her brows dipped and her lips curled into a frown.

"Yes. Who invited him here?"

"Fat Ma asked me to help you make amends with your father. I didn't ask any questions. I just told her I would. I invited him over for dinner. Fat Ma is coming too."

I walked off while she was in the middle of talking.

"This nigga getting the fuck out," I snarled to myself as I walked furiously into the living room of our home.

I had taken a quick trip to Atlanta, and I came back to this bullshit family fuckin' dinner that Cash was trying to pull off. Charles was tripping if he ever thought that we would be on some cool shit. He was the reason my mother had been murdered and my sister committed suicide. There was no coming back from that.

"You gotta go," I said to my father as he sat on the couch in the living room watching TV like shit was sweet.

He went to speak but stopped.

Cash had furiously rounded the corner.

"Wolf, stop. Mr. Charles, you don't have to go anywhere."

I looked away from Cash slowly. I would never harm a hair on her head, but I would beat the bullshit out anybody else for playing with me. My father was no exception.

"You already know what time it is. Don't let my girl get you killed in here. You and I both know how shit work with you and me. I asked you to leave. I won't ask again."

I stared at him with murder in my eyes. I was counting to three and if he let me get that far, I was going to break his jaw. I got to two and he was already up and scurrying from the living room and toward the door.

"We're moving," I said flatly as I stared at her blankly.

I was furious and I usually got quiet when I was angry, until I met Cash anyway.

"What is wrong with you? Are you that fuckin' hateful!" she spat as she sped behind me while I walked up the stairs toward our bedroom to pack a bag.

I didn't answer her question, I simply told her that she needed to pack a bag too. There was no way that we were staying up in there now that my father knew where we rested our heads.

"Wolf, I'm not going anywhere!" she said defiantly.

I stopped packing and then looked at her as she stood there angrily. Her arms were folded into her chest and her lip quivered. She was mad and rightfully so. She always talked about how she'd give anything to have her family intact. How she'd give her last to have another chance with her dad. I felt every word she said, but that shit didn't apply to me. I wanted to tell her so bad. Tell her why I hated him so much. I glared at her, and my jaws clenched. I was on the verge of telling her. It couldn't hurt anything.

"You are. Now get your shit," I told her before hopping on my phone to book us a suite.

* * *

"Hey stranger. It's been a minute since you decided to drop in. Guess they not important no more."

My brows instantly dipped at the sarcasm Tara was displaying. Her comment was giving off some weird ass signs of jealousy.

"So ..."

"So? What?"

I looked at Tara, lost. I wasn't sure what the fuck she wanted to know, but whatever it was, I wanted her to spit it out.

"So, Sin told me you had a new boo."

I nodded. "Something like that."

Cash was more than my little boo. I fucked with her the long way.

"So, you weren't gonna tell anybody?"

I eyed her blankly. "I didn't know I had to. You'll meet her soon."

"You okay?" I asked Tara.

She had opened the door and wasn't looking like her usual self. Her hair was in a messy bun on top of her head and the sweatpants and wife beater she used as loungewear had seen better days.

My eyes scanned the living room as I walked in, and it was then that I knew something was up. Shit was looking all kinds of crazy. Tara's townhouse had a modern, open floor plan with minimal furniture purposefully. She usually kept it neat and tidy, but this particular day it was all kinds of fucked up. Dishes overflowed in the sink, cups and plates as well as their half-eaten contents.

"No, I'm not alright," Tara replied. "I just want answers," she said before going into the living room and plopping down on the couch. I followed behind her and eyed a fifth of Hennesy and a red cup that she was probably drinking it from.

Depression was getting to her, and it was becoming more and more evident each day. I understood that grief was different for everyone, and it came in many different waves, but we had to get her out of that shit. She had kids to raise. I would have loved to give her some closure about what happened to Cheese, but I was unable to do that.

"Come on, T. Not this shit again. We've been through this over and over. We went down there, and motherfuckers is acting like they don't know nothing. What you want us to do? Just go down there and start killing any and everybody?"

She looked at me with a smug look that said 'yes.'

"We can't do that, Tara. All we can do is sit back and wait until we hear something, but don't let depression consume you. You still got kids to take care of. Where are they anyway?" I asked, noticing it was unusually quiet in there.

"They at my mama house," she said. She grabbed the red cup and drank from it, confirming that it was the liquor.

"Well look, I just came to check on you and the kids. I'll be back by in a few days. Stop sitting cooped up in this house though. Get out or something. And stop sitting around drinking fuckin' Hennesy all day," I told her. "And clean the fuck up."

I stood to my feet.

"You sure got a lot of demands for someone who barely checks on us."

"Cut it out. I missed one week because I got a piece of a life now." I paused as she looked at me.

"When do I get to meet her?"

"You and the kids get to meet her soon. At Sin's birthday party in a few weeks."

"Oh shit. I forgot that was coming up."

"You better not," I laughed. "You know how that nigga is about his birthday. He'll never let you hear the end of it. Get ya mom to watch the kids and pull up."

"I'll be there."

"Good. And make sure you get something done to that head. Don't bring yo' ass out looking like Don King."

"Fuck you, Wolf," she said, a smile creeping to her face.

"That's my girl. Show that beautiful smile. Fuck all that sad shit."

I leaned down to hug her before heading through the door.

"And make sure you wash yo' ass too. You living foul, girl!" I laughed, taking off just before she cursed me out.

Chapter 22
Cashmere "Cash" Ellis

Wolf shook violently. Sweat streamed down and flew off his face in specks as his body jerked. His eyes were shut, and he looked like he was having a nightmare.

"Babe! Babe!" I called as I shook him as hard as I could.

He was stuck in a deep trance, so I shook him harder until he stirred awake.

"Babe, you were having a nightmare," I told him.

His eyes fluttered and he looked around confused.

"Where are we?" he asked.

I eyed him with worry. This was the second night he'd done this shit. Since we'd been together, I noticed that he talked in his sleep, but he had never had a full-fledged nightmare until recently. Two nights in a row.

"We're at the hotel. Are you okay?"

"Not really, but I'll be okay," he said solemnly.

"No, talk about it, Wolf. I'll listen, babe. Tell me what's wrong. What's got you having nightmares?"

He exhaled a deep breath and sat quietly for several seconds.

"Please, Wolf. If it's something that I can help with, even if you just need someone to listen."

More silence until finally I went to lay back down. If he didn't want to talk about it, fine. I wasn't going to keep pressing the issue. But then he finally began speaking.

"Cash, I've done some horrible shit. Things I shouldn't have done. Shit so horrible ... the demons won't let me sleep in peace sometimes."

"Demons? Babe, what demons?" His words were scaring me.

"My demons," he said.

"We all have skeletons, Wolf."

"Not skeletons, babe. Demons." He looked at me with a dark coldness in his eyes that I'd never seen before, and it scared me a little.

"Well, what have you done, Wolf?"

"I know things. I've hurt people. Sometimes I do really evil shit. And I can't help it."

I bit down on my lip and studied him. I wasn't sure what to say.

"I need to know that you accept me as I am. That you're not gonna try to change me and then leave when the shit doesn't work. I love you and that's all I can promise you. That I'll love you. But I'm fucked up and I'll always be fucked up."

"Don't say that, baby."

He was rambling and the shit sounded borderline psychotic. I looked at the door and wondered how long would it take me to dash on his ass if he went batshit.

"I am. It's like once some evil shit sets in my mind, it won't go away. No matter who it's gonna hurt. No matter how wrong it seems. I can't control it. People aren't perfect and they're not always loyal, but I expect them to be. And when they aren't..." His voice trailed off.

"Would you hurt me?"

"I don't know," he said sadly. "I love you and I'd hope you never do no shit to give me the urge to hurt you. Because when those urges come, I can't control them."

"I love you too Wolf, and I wouldn't ever give you a reason to hurt me. And I don't care how dark your past is or how many secrets you have. I love you."

He'd said it first and I could finally tell him how I truly felt. I loved Wolf and I realized it the night that we had sex. I was glad that we waited because I now didn't just have a lover, I also had a best friend. I didn't see those demons that Wolf spoke of. I saw a genuine, loving man that was a little rough around the edges, but still a good person.

Wolf smiled at me but didn't say anything. I wasn't sure whether he believed me when I said that I loved him in spite of his demons or if he was unsure of whether those demons would overpower him to go against the love he had for me.

Chapter 23
Tara Jones

"Amya, getcho ass down from my chair!" I screamed out at the top of my lungs from where I was standing in the kitchen making breakfast.

Out of all my children, her little ass was the fucking worst! Actually, let me rephrase that, because I loved my kids with all my heart, but she was bad as hell. Long kinky hair that I kept in ponytails, and smooth, beautiful, caramel skin, Amya was my only girl. Loving but because she was raised underneath two brothers, she acted just like them. And after five years on earth, she had actually become rougher than her brothers.

My boys Amir and Amar were typical boys. With their shiny, dark-chocolate skin, they looked just like their mama. Amya was her father's twin. She had his mannerisms, his temperament, and would turn up just like him.

Thoughts of Cheese instantly brought tears to my eyes. I didn't understand how a ruthless ass nigga like him could let niggas get out on him. Cheese was 'bout that life and had real motion. A true millionaire in the drug game.

He and I had been together for eight years and in that time, he had done nothing but make my life better. He wanted a house full of kids and was all about family. He'd been missing for 339 days, and no day was easy. The shit didn't get better as the days passed. I had no closure and that made it even harder.

"Girl, stop yelling at my damn niece," my sister Paulita grumbled into the phone, pulling me out of my thoughts. I had forgotten that I was even on the phone.

"Girl please. You know Amya is bad. I done told her a hundred times not to jump on my couch."

"*Not a hundred*," my sister countered sarcastically. Amya was her baby, and, in her eyes, she could do no wrong.

I was the only sister with kids. After having two boys, everybody had their fingers crossed for a girl and was excited when I found out that was what I was having. She was spoiled rotten on top of her naturally bad ass ways. To put it mildly, Amya was something else.

"Yes, bitch. Literally a hundred. Maybe two hundred. She broke the lamp in the living room last week and just a few weeks ago, she blacked Amar's eye from a remote she threw at him. Baby girl is out of control."

"You need a break. Let's go out.

When I first met Cheese, I was a party animal. A club was where I actually met him.

"Girl, you know I'm not going out to no club. I ain't fucked with the club since Cheese."

"Yeah, that didn't stop his ass though," my sister said bitterly. They never cared for Cheese, but I wasn't trying to hear that negative shit, especially because he was still missing, and my mental state was getting worse by the day. The bitch was uncaring like that.

"Well, how about we go shopping?" she asked. "You know a little retail therapy always made a bitch feel good."

I wasn't sure if she meant me or herself, but I agreed. After calling my mama up to watch my bad ass kids, I took off and met my sister at the mall so I could blow some of Sin and Wolf's bread on me and her thirsty ass.

* * *

"You know her?" my sister Paulita asked with a frown.

We were at Saks on Peachtree Road browsing the Chanel section. Apparently Paulita must have caught a bitch staring at us, because her face was turned up and now looking in the direction of where three broads were standing. Two of the women whispered and stood around one, who stood with both arms wrapped around the baby that she was carrying on her hip.

"Nah," I said softly.

I knew how quickly shit could escalate so I chose not to jump to conclusions. I didn't know either of those hoes but apparently, one of them knew me and low-key looked like she wanted smoke. The one holding the baby kept glaring at me while the others whispered. I didn't say anything in an effort to keep my temper in line.

While I went back to browsing through the Chanel products on display, Paulita continued to steal glances in the direction of the hostile-looking women. However, Paulita went on defense, and I stopped browsing when they began walking toward us.

"Do I know you?" I asked before shorty holding the baby could say anything. The three of them had just pulled right up on us.

"No, you don't, but Cheese does."

I swallowed the rock-hard lump in my throat. I knew some bullshit was about to come. I was one of the sweetest people you could meet, but when I lost my temper, all hell was finna break loose.

"Okay, and what that gotta do with me?" I asked her, inadvertently matching her tone.

Shit was about to go left. The bullshit reminded me of my younger days when I was always in the streets scrapping with Paulita and our other sister, Kyra.

I was never a bitch of many words. I was from zone six and when bitches went left, I would quickly gather them together and bring them back right. Even though Wolf told me to lay off the Hennesy, I hadn't listened. I'd continued to sip on my bottle of brown trouble and now its effects were about to fuel my actions.

"It got a lot to do with you since you his wife and this his baby. That nigga done disappeared and somebody got to kick out some cash for mine. You and his mama got all the money while my baby ain't got shit."

My eyes lowered into slits, while my mouth stiffened. Even in its tightened state, my lips quivered in anger. With the red-bottom stiletto still in my hand, I lunged at her. I had so much pent-up frustration in me. So much rage. I blacked out, disregarding the fact that the bitch was still holding her baby.

"You okay?" Sin asked.

I was sitting quietly in the passenger seat, staring blankly out the window.

"Yeah," I replied quietly, not bothering to turn my head to address him.

"No you're not. Say what's on ya mind."

He was right. I wasn't okay. I was not only humiliated, but I was depleted mentally.

"You knew about that shit?" I asked, finally turning away from the window and facing Sin's snake ass.

"Yeah, I did. But it wasn't my place to tell you," he admitted.

I scoffed and shook my head. I now saw how he was rocking. I wasn't sure why I was shocked. He wasn't my blood relative. He was Cheese's. That's where his loyalty lie and he made that shit crystal ball clear.

"Wasn't your place, huh. Tell me Sin, what the fuck else you know about but ain't telling me? You know what happened to Cheese? Is the nigga dead or what?" I snapped.

"I don't know shit else, T. You knew like everybody else that Cheese wasn't a fuckin' saint. Yeah, he took care of his family, but saying the nigga was loyal would be a stretch. That's the nigga you chose," he reminded me sharply.

"We supposed to be family. Cheese been missing for nearly a fucking year. I'm his wife. His legal spouse. If that nigga got illegitimate kids out here, what's stopping them bitches from coming after me?"

Senator sat quietly, stared at the road, and focused on driving.

"I didn't think about that," he finally said after about a minute of silence.

"Clearly," I muttered bitterly. "For all I know that nigga was down in Tennessee fucking a bitch and got set up. It would be just like his ass to go out like that."

"Nah. If Cheese was fucking anyone, I would have known about it. He did his dirt, but he was cautious. He didn't fuck around with hood bitches. The hoes he hit, worked. Had shit going for themselves. I mean, you were a stretch."

"The fuck is that supposed to mean?" I snapped.

"I mean, you were a hood chick. You partied and bullshit and made bad fucking choices. Hence the reason why you beat the fuck out of shorty when she told you she had a baby by Cheese. She ain't swing on you or threaten you! And she had her fuckin' baby in her arms that she dropped. You lucky the baby didn't get hurt."

"She had it coming. She was with her homegirls, and she tried to embarrass me."

"It don't matter, T. You're a mother. Not only are you above them bitches, you're all those kids got for real now. You can't be out here jeopardizing your freedom like them kids don't depend on you. What? You want them with your mom or sister if something happen to you?"

"Fuck that shit, Sin. The bitch fucked my husband knowing full damn well that he was married. Then pop up telling me she had his baby and need help. The audacity! I ain't got no fucking sympathy for them hoes. Every day is a struggle for me. Cheese was nowhere near perfect, but he was my partner. The nigga that I thought I would spend the rest of my life with. He's gone, and I have no answers. And it's not like you or Wolf are doing shit about it."

Sin didn't respond. He just sat there looking angry while my words seemed to sink in.

"Why the fuck is that, Sin?"

"We don't have no leads, T."

"Yeah, well maybe neither of you are niggas trying hard enough."

I was frustrated and I was borderline bitter. I'd just got booked, processed, and bonded out for putting hands and feet on the hoe that came to me in Saks. I was to the point where I didn't give a fuck if they locked me up for the shit or not. I wasn't giving that bitch a dime of nothing I had or that Cheese had left for me. And if Sin and Wolf didn't find out soon what happened to Cheese, then I was going to be taking matters into my own hands.

Chapter 24
Blanca Lopez

I'd made some mistakes in my life, but as I looked down into the chubby, smiling face of my baby boy, EJ, I told myself that he wasn't one of them. He had features like his daddy, but he would deny that. The main reason being I had slept with one of his closest friends one drunken night. I didn't mean to hurt him. Had I known he was so fragile, I would have tread lightly and proceeded with caution. But I didn't, now one person was dead and me, well, I'd paid the ultimate price. The guilt of knowing I was the reason for a man's death. The scars from the beating I took, and the life of my son that could never be lived to its fullest. He wanted to kill me. I could see it in his eyes. He'd started to. Fortunately, for me, something changed.

Wolf was good to me, but he was always gone. We'd met when he and his homeboy had come into the city to do business. I'll never forget it. We were at a club. I'd come from money, so I wasn't easily impressed. What impressed me was the man's character. He liked my zest. My fiery spirit. But what he missed was my rebellious spirit. My need for adventure and my tendency to break the rules. I wasn't from the streets, so I didn't believe in the code or none of that bullshit. I was just a neglected girlfriend that wanted her man's attention. But it went too far.

I'd given up my life for Wolf. I didn't grow up rich, but I'd come from a respectable Dominican family. A family who also happened to not approve of me dating a black man. I chose Wolf and when he left me, I went crawling back to the people that I'd given up over him. Needless to say, they weren't as receptive as I hoped them to be. Factoring in the fact that I returned seven months pregnant, really disappointed them. I was on my own and I had been struggling ever since. I had a special needs child, and the assistance that I was receiving for him wasn't going to cut it. Especially when his father was a rich man who was fully capable of providing him with a great life.

Wolf had told me that I was dead to him that day. He didn't want shit to do with me, and rightfully so. Deep in my heart, I believed that he had tried to beat the baby out of me so he wouldn't have any ties whatsoever. But it didn't happen that way. He probably had no idea that despite the beating I took, I still brought his child into the world. Well, that was definitely about to change. EJ needed more than I could give him, and I was going to see to it that he got everything he deserved. Or I was about to tell the people most important to him what had really happened to his best friend.

Also by Shontaiye Moore

The Trillest Boss Wifed The Baddest Chick 3

The Trillest Boss Wifed The Baddest Chick 2

The Trillest Boss Wifed The Baddest Chick

A Millionaire And A Project Chick

A Millionaire And A Project Chick 2

A Millionaire And A Project Chick 3

That D Hit Different When He Broke

That D Hit Different When He Broke 2

That D Hit Different When He Broke 3

The Rise Of A Dope Boy Chick

The Rise Of A Dope Boy Chick 2

The Autobiography Of A Project Chick

On Every Thug I Love

A Birmingham Thug Captured My Heart

Made in the USA
Monee, IL
03 October 2023

43894632R00102